PR

MW00773644

JOAQUIM MARIA MACHADO DE ASSIS

"The kind of humor that makes skulls smile."

—Salman Rushdie

"A great ironist, a tragic comedian. . . . In his books, in their most comic moments, he underlines the suffering by making us laugh."

—Philip Roth

"The greatest writer ever produced in Latin America."

—Susan Sontag

"The supreme black literary artist to date."

—Harold Bloom

"Machado de Assis is Brazil's greatest novelist, and ranks high among the most appealing writers in the world. . . . Though he lived mainly in the nineteenth century, Machado possesses an almost postmodern sensibility—playful, ironic and tricky."

—Michael Dirda, *Washington Post Book World*

"Machado de Assis was a literary force, transcending nationality and language."

—*New York Times Book Review*

"No satirist, not even Swift, is less merciful in his exposure of the pretentiousness and the hypocrisy that lurk in the average good man and woman."

—*New Republic*

Selected Books by Joaquim Maria Machado de Assis

Joaquim Maria Machado de Assis

RESURRECTION

Translated by Karen C. Sherwood Sotelino

Introduction by José Luiz Passos

DALKEY ARCHIVE PRESS
Dallas / Dublin

Translation copyright © by Karen Sherwood Sotelino, 2013, 2021
Introduction copyright © by José Luiz Passos, 2013, 2021

First Dalkey Archive edition, 2021

Library of Congress Cataloguing-in-Publication Data Available
ISBN: 9781628973846

www.dalkeyarchive.com
Dallas / Dublin

Printed on permanent/durable acid-free paper.

Table of Contents

Resurrection: Machado de Assis's Debut Novel

I

Joaquim Maria Machado de Assis (1839-1908) made his debut in the novel genre with an apparently unpretentious book. *Resurrection* (1872) was published two and a half years after originally anticipated and, like *Dom Casmurro* (1899), seems to have had a slow maturation. Of the first seven novels published by the author, only these two were not serialized in periodicals. The contract, signed on September 30, 1869 with editor B. L. Garnier, was optimistic and bound the author to a genre that was still foreign to him. In 1872, when his first novel finally came out, Machado de Assis had already published six other works of poetry, drama, and short stories: *Desencantos* (Disenchantments, 1861), *Teatro* (Theater, 1863), *Crisálidas* (Chrysalides, 1864), *Os deuses de casaca* (Gods in Suits, 1866), in addition to *Falenas* (Moths) and *Contos fluminenses* (Short Stories from Rio), both published in 1870.

Contrary to the contemporary trend in Brazil, in his

first novel Machado de Assis opted to depict the intimate conflict between two protagonists threatened by the
shadow of past romantic experiences. *Resurrection* develops
a new theme: the scrutiny of the *other* from the point of
view of someone who lives in self-deception—a bold idea
for the pen of a novice in the genre. But in the case of
Machado de Assis, boldness was almost always rewarded
with the currency of praise, and I believe this is in part
due to the manner with which his innovations were always
anchored in the full confidence that the author placed in
the long literary tradition that preceded him.

Resurrection avoids the typical raptures and pitfalls of
Brazilian Romanticism. Although the theme is romantic—the deceit rooted in the incredulous heart of a misanthrope—its realization was substantially new for its attempt
to infuse moral verisimilitude through introspection. It
thus departed from a standard whose emphasis remained
on fanciful plots and descriptions of the national landscape.
Doctor Félix resists the possibility of overcoming his distrust in mankind—and, therefore, resists love—because
he assumes the *possibility* of betrayal on the part of his
fiancée, the young widow Lívia, to be *full proof* of her
future behavior toward him. In his debut novel, Machado
de Assis already makes verisimilitude and veracity con-
verge deceptively, announcing a premise that would later
mark almost all of his novels. In the end, Félix remains
without any remorse; he dismisses the possibility of Lívia's
innocence simply because she seems dubious to him.
Félix seeks parallels and confirmation in literature and
other art forms. He follows the suggestions of a rival for
Lívia's affections, a man who leads him toward the realm

of doubt, imitating Iago—the famous villain in *Othello*. Félix's inability to justly assess his fiancée's moral character hinders the possibility of a second love and condemns both to disenchantment. As a point of departure for this work, Machado de Assis opted for an unusual affiliation, and made a rare declaration of his authorial intentions in the Preface to the first edition:

> My idea when I wrote this book was to put into practice Shakespeare's thought:
>
> *Our doubts are traitors,*
> *And make us lose the good we oft might win,*
> *By fearing to attempt.*
>
> I did not want to write a novel of manners: I have tried to sketch a situation and to contrast two characters; with these simple elements I have tried to make the book interesting.

The quote from *Measure for Measure* establishes the novel within an approach that fascinated Machado de Assis: works that consider the moral consequences of obsessive love, works that engender dramas characterized by a counterpoint between jealousy, resentment, and remorse, often unbeknownst to the protagonist. Machado de Assis is probably citing *Measure for Measure* from the only collection of Shakespeare's complete works in English that he had (*The Handy-Volume Shakspeare*, 13 vols., London, Bradbury, Evans, and Co., 1868, vol. 2, I.i.77-79). A collation between his citations and the text of this edition coincides in practically all cases. On at least one occasion, Machado de Assis adopts an unorthodox spelling of the playwright's name, clearly following the title of the collection he owned, which shows "Shakspeare" instead of "Shakespeare." From the play he also explores the theme of justice threatened by suspicion, which defines a protagonist who lacks in self-knowledge.

II

The opening of *Resurrection* exemplifies a new psychological approach to the qualms and quandaries of a hero whose sense of self is at stake:

> That day—ten years ago, so quickly passed!—Doctor Félix got up late, opened the window, greeting the sun. It was a splendid day. A cool ocean breeze approached, gently breaking into the scorching summer. A few sparse, small white clouds, thin and transparent, stood out from the azure sky. Chirping in the garden next door to the doctor's house there were several birds, accustomed to the semi-urban, semi-sylvan life Laranjeiras had to offer. It seemed all of nature was collaborating to start out the year. If the exuberance of bygone years had been washed away for some, others still recalled the passions of their childhood and adolescence in hailing this day.Everything seems better, more beautiful to us—the result of our illusion—that our joy in welcoming the New Year precludes our noticing it is also a step toward death.

Would this last idea have seeped into Félix's soul as he contemplated the magnificent, splendorous bright sky? Certainly, a fleeting cloud seemed to cross his forehead. Félix's gaze absorbed the horizon. He remained still and engrossed for a long while, as if he were questioning the future or turning over the past. Then, with a gesture of ennui and, seemingly embarrassed for having ceded to chimeric contemplation, he descended quickly into prose, lit a cigar, and waited peacefully for his luncheon. (Chapter I)

The wistful and ironic tone, in the very first two paragraphs, reveals a trait that years later would come to be identified with Machado de Assis's style. From the beginning, loss marks the world of the hero and undermines any promise of deliverance or restoration. Merging shade with sun, dissolution with rejoicing, Machado de Assis opens a world where all contentment engenders its own disillusionment—a valid insight to his overall canon. The possibility of "resurrection" becomes in fact aborted, confirming the prefiguration set by the closure of the first paragraph.

The humble tone of the Preface contrasts with the boldness of the theme. *Resurrection* is a novel about the doubt that devastates the hero's heart and victimizes the object of his affections. From the outset, the narrator draws on the opposition between the past and the present, the light and the dark, and between the rural and the urban. In this manner, he also outlines the moral character of Félix, whose inner life is overwhelmed with hesitations and conflicting feelings.

How does an author create characters possessing the

complex and contradictory dimension of a moral person? Machado de Assis seems to have achieved this through visual metaphors and the sinuous relationship that the protagonists maintain with the burden of their pasts and, interestingly, also with the use that they make of artworks.

Resurrection has a simple plot. Despite his fear of commitment, Doctor Félix falls in love with the beautiful Lívia, a young melancholic widow. She reciprocates his affections and the pair begins a love affair marked from the start by Felix's uncertainty as to both his capacity and willingness to love her *fully*. The plot is thickened by the presence of three characters that float around the relationship between the doctor and the widow: Raquel, a languid teen in love with Félix; Meneses, a friend of his and an admirer of Lívia; and Luís Batista, a flighty adventurer, who despite being married, quarrels with Félix over the widow. At the insistence of Félix himself, the relationship of the couple is kept secret and the marriage is delayed more than once. However, Félix is not merely a simple emanation of typical romantic fickleness. One of his main character traits is his ability to conceal his motives, which enables him to love Lívia and evade public opinion at the same time as he nurtures his possessive and distrustful nature.

Félix encounters Lívia for the first time in the third chapter, at an evening soirée. The fascination of the first impression extends to the intrusion of the narrator, which to this point in the novel has been limited to relatively short descriptions of characters and their bonds. The two waltz. At the side of the widow, the doctor finds himself "oblivious to the comments of others, entirely given over to the fancy of his own thoughts":

Nonetheless in mid-conversation, he escaped—I'm not certain with which phrase of melancholic skepticism—leaving the young woman disquieted. Lívia looked at him, then to the floor, seemingly so absorbed she did not even notice the silence that ensued, following her gesture and Félix's words. He took advantage of the situation to examine her more fully. [. . .] Her smooth, wide brow would seemingly never be troubled by reflection. Nevertheless, anyone examining the young woman's face at that instant would see she was no stranger to inner strife: her lively eyes had moments of languor. On that occasion they were neither alive nor languid. They were still.

It seemed as if she were looking with her spirit. (Chapter III)

Waltzing, Félix is preoccupied with himself; a stray comment on his part unleashes an introspective fervor in Lívia that deepens the silence between the two—a type of silence of which she herself will soon be ashamed. It is characteristic of this novel that the eyes lower to remain *seeing*, and that speechlessness reveals vast interior worlds driven by self-inspection and scrutiny of the other. Introspection immobilizes the gaze, vitrifies it. It is through the eyes that the silent love between Félix and Lívia is explained and expressed: the gaze becomes reflexive, for example, when responding to Félix's restrained and anticlimactic declaration of love, Lívia suddenly "drank from his eyes a long look of gratitude and elation" (Chapter VI). Just as at the end of the paragraph cited above, the gaze extends to stand for the concept of a moral person. After the exchange of loving vows, the hero is described alone, in silent soliloquy, even though he is among many people, including his own lover. His alienation from the external world is foregrounded as soon as he begins to reflect upon the nature of his feelings. Félix "heard himself. He contemplated the scene with envious delight, feeling a pang of regret"; "Emotion blocked his voice, reflection governed his silence"; "it seemed as if some sort of vague and remote idea surfaced in his soul, making a long excursion through the field of his memory". "With this fantasy, he drafted a future existence"; "By the time Félix arrived home, he was entirely convinced that the widow's affection was a mixture of vanity, caprice, and sensual inclination." In the space of a few hours—and two chapters—on the way home after declaring his love to Lívia, Félix radically changes his mind about the sincerity of the widow's love, with absolutely nothing having occurred to provoke this change of heart.

As soon as the doctor delves into an interior world, the evocation of the past unleashes a former penchant for mistrust. Félix looks down upon a sincere and selfless love because of his inability to believe in the sincerity of others. It is suggestive that he, when faced with Lívia's love, is ashamed of his own fickleness: "When the widow's eyes sought out those of the doctor, the latter would cautiously avert his; but then he would look, shall we say, from beneath his lids" (Chapter VIII). Gazing from beneath the eyelids—this metaphor of moral vision that denounces the subject attentive to the other, while at the same time peering back, will come to define much of the difference that brands the Machadian hero's confidence. We return to the value judgment that infuses the gaze with the specific weight of a brooding shame. Like Lívia, the doctor also gazes from the soul: "Félix's love had a bitter taste, laced with doubt and suspicion" (Chapter IX). His capriciousness and skepticism come from a past deception in a love relationship. Faced with Lívia's confrontation—which reveals her to be a frustrated and demanding dreamer—Félix responds that he has lost much more than a great love: "While I, my dear Lívia, lack the principle element of inner peace, for I don't trust in the sincerity of others" (Chapter XI). Félix seems to apply this rule to the widow herself. He suggests the idea that failed affective relations morally transform the character of people. But if unrestricted distrust is a burden on one's relationship with the other, how does he form new judgments about the other?

III

Let us briefly consider how the protagonists relate to imagined events and to worlds of fiction and art. I believe that part of the response can be found here, and that this same trait will later come to define Machado de Assis's most well-known protagonists.

At the outset of the novel, Félix breaks off, "with no sense of loss or pity," a relationship because of boredom and a lack of trust in love; but the break-up is rationalized "also because Félix had just read a book by Henri Murger, in which he had discovered a character prone to impetuous catastrophe. The woman of his thoughts, as a poet would say, thus received a *coup*, both moral and literary" (Chapter

I). The hero fully equates his soul with that of the fictional character. Verisimilitude provides him with reinforcement for a decision about his relationship with others. The doctor mimics the book that he reads. In fact, at the precise moment when Félix ends his relationship with Cecília—another possible fiancée—he encounters her seated, reading as well. Félix approaches her, takes the book from her hands and refers to the situation between them, about to be extinguished, as a short, concluded chapter. He then leaves to unveil another fantasy world: that of the young widow who had already captivated his imagination.

Lívia too, according to her own brother Viana, suffers from a similar syndrome: "she's a romantic. Her head's filled with intrigue, the natural fruit of the solitude she's experienced these past two years, in addition to the books she must have read" (Chapter I). Both are immature readers. On another occasion, Félix observes Lívia's transparent reactions to the enactment of a romantic drama. Félix believes that in Lívia's eyes he reads the reversal of a hidden emotion, forced to the surface by the frenzy of the melodrama they had seen. The examples are numerous. Since the true meaning of human motives is disguised by dissimulation and politeness, Félix believes the world needs to be constantly *interpreted*. Even gestures and touches, like the grasp of hands between the protagonists at the end of the waltz in chapter IV, are riddled with subterfuge and need to be clarified by observations, contrasts, and comparisons. Félix's preferred means is frequently that of the exegete who seeks, in his own past or in works of art, terms to clarify unspoken intentions—his own, and those of others as well.

Luís Batista knows this and awakens the hero's penchant for delusional imaginings. The doctor's misogynistic distrust is nurtured by the maliciousness of his opponent. The rival in this courtship with Lívia is aware of the nature of Félix's love and intends to use this inclination to dissolve the couple's relationship:

> To obtain this result, it was necessary to multiply the doctor's suspicions, carve the jealous wound deeply into his heart, transform him, in sum, into the instrument of his own ruin. Luís Batista did not adopt Iago's method, which struck him as risky and childish. Instead of insinuating suspicion into Félix's ears, he placed it before his eyes. (Chapter IX)

Luís Batista's plan works. Regardless of his own suspicions and pressured by the interest of another suitor, Félix schedules a date for the wedding that ends up not taking place; once more, Félix flees the scene without any apparent reason. The villain had sent an anonymous letter to the groom-to-be affirming that, just as with the first husband, Félix too would be victimized by Lívia's fickle nature. To dispel suspicions about himself, Luís Batista makes a visit to Félix at the same moment that the latter receives the letter. The rival's call is under the pretext of shopping for an engraving representing the theme of lust and betrayal, in which King David peers at the young Bathsheba during her bath. In the conversation between the two, the metaphor of life as opera—a metaphor later developed extensively in *Dom Casmurro*—is used by Luís Batista to explain the doctor's situation. With an imagination saturated by his own eyes, Félix convinces himself of Lívia's guilt. Only at the end of the novel does his friend Meneses finally seem to persuade him otherwise. Plagued by the doubt of his own judgment, the doctor returns and begs forgiveness from the widow, who no longer accepts him. The link between *seeing* and *imagining* is a way of making the protagonists acquire inner depth; this extension resorts to fantasy worlds that summarize the conscience and the predicaments of the hero.

The conclusion of the novel returns to Shakespeare's play and reinforces the combination between distrust of the other, self-deception, and the imagining of possible malicious conduct. For Félix, as well as for Bento Santiago, in *Dom Casmurro*, verisimilitude is often the whole of truth:

> The doctor's love experienced posthumous doubts. With the passing of years, the veracity of the letter that had prevented their marriage not only seemed possible to him, but even probable. One day Meneses told Félix he had ultimate proof that Luís Batista had written the letter. Not only did Félix refuse his testimony, he didn't even ask what proof he had. He thought to himself that, even without Batista's vileness, the verisimilitude of fact could not be excluded, and that alone assured him of his rectitude. (Chapter XXIV)

Resurrection is certainly no exception to the romantic novel. Yet, in contrast to many other narratives of the period, the objective was to emphasize the contrast and the development of the moral person through love lost due to an obsession with the *possibility* of betrayal. Prior this novel, there are

nearly fifty references to Shakespeare to be found throughout Machado de Assis's body of work. He was familiar with
Shakespeare's work mostly through French translations,
like those of Émile Montégut published between the late
1860s and early 1870s. Having discarded the possibility of
"a novel of manners" as a model for his debut in the genre,
Machado de Assis explored, possibly for the first time in
Brazilian fiction, the theme of a consciousness in disagreement with itself; a dissent caused by the shadow of past
events. The motif of fickleness and weakness of will marked
many of Machado de Assis's first short stories, and they
reveal his interest in misanthropy and heroes derailed by
moral inertia. In fact, the social types of the misanthrope,
the libertine, and the sensual adventurer—three major
threats to the constitution of the bourgeois family—are
frequent in the short stories that Machado de Assis regu-
larly published in the *Jornal das Famílias*, a monthly mag-
azine published in Rio de Janeiro by the French editor B.
L. Garnier. Machado de Assis contributed to this periodical
from 1864 to 1878 with short stories of a predominantly
moralizing nature. The characters of the misanthrope and
the libertine stand out as ideal types for the moral example because of their deviant behavior, sometimes retreating
from society, other times embracing it through vice. Two
solutions often fit these figures: moral conversion after marriage, as is the case with Jorge in "O caminho de Damasco"
(The Way to Damascus), published in November, 1871; or
the solution of segregation, as is expressed by the suicide
of Luís Soares in the homonymous short story, published
in 1864 and subsequently included in the volume *Contos
fluminenses* in 1870. Written at the time of these short

stories, *Resurrection* is a more psychologically profound
development of the same social types.

However, while in the first phase of Machado de Assis's
work fickleness is a moral defect that the narrative will
punish through isolation or irony, in his second phase this
trait comes to dominate the plot and the moral makeup
of the narrator himself, providing him with a method and
the advantage of perspective over other characters and the
world at large.

IV

In conclusion, Machado de Assis refined his skills in ren-
dering morally complex characters throughout his first four
novels, published between 1872 and 1878. They depict by
and large the social integration and compromises of young
women, orphans, and dependents of the elite families of
the Brazilian Second Reign (1840–1889). Shame and dissimulation come to the fore; both are at the root of the
Machadian concept of a moral person. His characters still
find themselves subjected to the integrating force of the
romantic plot that sought to reconcile opposing tensions
to ensure, finally, the union of a couple through the formation of a new family. However, even within this context,
the protagonists of these first four novels are affected by a
new kind of deficit: by a sensation of guilt or a spurious
desire that distances them, little by little, from prototypical
romantic characters. They relentlessly seek to overcome a
primordial state of humiliation through a calculated and
socially ascendant trajectory. Thus, the formation of the

new bourgeois family in the novels of Machado de Assis's first phase is linked to the unique capacity of dissimulation that his characters possess, masking their motives and origins. The failed relationship between Lívia and Félix, in *Resurrection*, is a compendium of motifs that made Machado de Assis's fiction dissonant within the contemporaneous Portuguese and Brazilian canon—where there was a virtual absence of well-to-do protagonists characterized as misanthropic, skeptical, sly and misogynistic, unable to form a family due to fickleness and lack of will.

Early reviews highlight the exceptional nature of the novel. Comparing Machado de Assis to his contemporaries, José Carlos Rodrigues, the editor of *O Novo Mundo* (a Brazilian liberal periodical published in New York during the 1870s), commented that, among the writers and critics of the time, he was considered "more of an artist" than his competitors. José Carlos Rodrigues also underscored what he perceived to be a difference of aim and achievement between Machado de Assis's narratives and those of his contemporaries. Machado de Assis soon came to represent a third path within the Brazilian novelistic form—in addition to Romanticism and Naturalism. Part of this can be explained by his distinct way of composing protagonists and justifying their motivations. In *Resurrection*, Machado de Assis initiated his depiction of dynamic inner lives, characters whose personas are in a constant state of revision and self-doubt—a technique that will culminate in the self-consciously romantic realism of *Yaya Garcia* (1878).

For the reader of today, who is likely to enter the world of Machado de Assis through *The Posthumous Memoirs of Brás Cubas* (1881), *Quincas Borba* (1891), or *Dom Casmurro* (1899), *Resurrection* represents an unusual debut: Félix anticipates the volubility of Brás Cubas, the tenuous moral character of Rubião, and Bento Santiago's tyrannical jealousy. In one of the passages cited above, Machado de Assis makes Shakespeare appear once more, when the narrative identifies Luís Batista with an Iago that, through the eyes of the doctor, intensifies the doubt of a heart already predisposed to suspicion. As I have pointed out, one of the crucial results of the interference of this Brazilian Iago is Félix's insistence on judging the *possible* actions of Lívia based on her *likely* past actions. Félix distrusts the widow and, to assure himself of his doubts, he revisited all the goings on of the previous days, never more convinced of the young woman's treachery, nor of the misery of his own soul" (Chapter IX), exactly as Bento Santiago does almost thirty years later in his autobiography at the turn of the twentieth century.

From *Resurrection* on, Machado de Assis found in some of Shakespeare's plays a language and set of dramatic episodes that enact a search for the troubled unity of the protagonist's fractured self. In key moments of at least seven out of his nine novels, when Machado de Assis's protagonists or narrators face obstacles linked to the qualms and quandaries of their consciences, they resort to direct quotes, allusions, or parodies of Shakespeare in order to overcome what is usually an unavoidable sense of shame or guilt. These references are used to deepen or clarify Machado de Assis's characterization of inwardness. In every single case, the moral sentiments at play—emotions of self-assessment such as guilt, pride, shame, remorse, or jealousy—constitute the main object of his novels, and respond to social issues debated at the time of their writing. Taken as a whole, these narratives show that even in contexts where agents believe they are constrained by a deterministic framework, free will and imputation of culpability are not necessarily precluded. This insight was essential to Machado de Assis's social critique of society immediately prior to the Brazilian abolition of slavery (1888) and the advent of the Republic (1889), when Social Darwinism and Positivism shaped the worldview of the Brazilian intelligentsia. Machado de Assis's narratives articulate an effective indictment of how determinism undermines agency and impacts the representation of personhood and agency in the public sphere. In this context, psychological depth becomes a consequential make-believe game we play with and take pleasure in when we read his novels. And, in many ways, everything began with *Resurrection*.

By José Luiz Passos
University of California, Los Angeles

Translated by Kevin G. McDonald

Preface to the New Edition

This was my first novel, written many years ago. In this new edition, I have altered neither the composition, nor the style. I have merely changed one or two words, and corrected spelling, here and there. Along with others that followed, and a few short stories and novellas, this novel belongs to the first phase of my literary life.

M. de A.
1905

Preface to the First Edition

I do not know what to think of this book. Above all, I will ignore what the reader will think. The generous reception of my volume of short stories and novellas, published two years ago, encouraged me to write it. It is an attempt. It goes unpretentiously into the hands of the critics and public, who will treat it with whatever justice it deserves.

Critics are always suspicious of modest prologues, and they are right. Generally, they are like the exaggerated claims of an elegant woman, who sees or believes herself to be pretty, and thus wishes to emphasize her natural graces. I flee, crossing myself three times, when faced with one of those contrite, disingenuous prefaces, composed with eyes lowered toward the dust of humility and the heart set at the peak of ambition. If you see only the eyes, and venture to speak the painful truth, you risk sinking in the author's opinion, in spite of his self-proclaimed humility and his request for honesty.

Well, I dare tell the fine and stern critics that this preface is entirely unlike those others. I come presenting an attempt, in a genre new to me, and I wish to know if some quality calls me to it, or if I am lacking them all—in which case, since I have worked somewhat successfully in other fields, I will turn my attention and efforts elsewhere. All I ask of the critics is that they be well-intentioned, frank and just. Applause, with no basis in merit, certainly nourishes the spirit and provides celebrity with some veneer, but anyone who wants to learn and to create anything prefers a lesson of improvement to the din of flattery.

When extremely young, we expect too much from ourselves, and nothing or nearly nothing seems laborious or impossible. But, time, that great teacher, corrodes such confidence, leaving us with only that which is indispensable to mankind, doing away with all the rest—evil and blinding confidence. With time, thought reigns over its own empire, and time must include study, without which the spirit remains forever childish.

Later the opposite occurs. The greater our familiarity with the models, the more we reach the depths of taste and art, and the more our hands and spirit hesitate. Yet, this very situation stimulates our ambition—no longer presumptuous, but thoughtful. This is perhaps not the law of genius, those endowed by nature with a nearly unconscious power of extreme daring, but it is, I believe, the law of the average mind, the general rule for minimal intelligence.

I have already reached this point. Although thankful for the kind words with which benevolent judges have encouraged me, I still hesitate greatly. Each day I have renewed appreciation for the arduousness of the literary task, which is surely noble and consoling, though difficult when carried out conscientiously.

When I wrote this book, my idea was to put into practice Shakespeare's thought:

Our doubts are traitors,
and make us lose the good we oft might win,
By fearing to attempt.

I did not want to write a novel of manners. I have tried
to depict a situation and to contrast two characters. With
these simple elements I have tried to make the book interesting. Critics will decide if the work fulfills its intentions,
and above all, if the worker has a skill for it.

This is what I ask of them, with my heart in my hands.

M. de A.

Resurrection

I

New Year's Day

That day—ten years ago, so quickly passed!—Doctor Félix[1] got up late, opened the window, greeting the sun. It was a splendid day. A cool ocean breeze approached, gently breaking into the scorching summer. A few sparse, small white clouds, thin and transparent, stood out from the azure sky. Chirping in the garden next door to the doctor's house there were several birds, accustomed to the semi-urban, semi-sylvan life Laranjeiras[2] had to offer. It seemed all of nature was collaborating to start out the year. If the exuberance of bygone years had been washed away for some, others still recalled the passions of their childhood and adolescence in hailing this day. Everything seems better, more beautiful—the result of our illusion—our joy in welcoming the New Year precludes our noticing it is also a step toward death.

Would this last idea have seeped into Félix's soul as he contemplated the magnificent, splendorous bright sky? Certainly, a fleeting cloud seemed to cross his forehead. Félix's gaze absorbed the horizon. He remained still and engrossed for a long while, as if he were questioning the future or turning over the past. Then, with a gesture of ennui and, seemingly embarrassed for having ceded to chimeric contemplation, he descended quickly into prose, lit a cigar, and waited peacefully for his luncheon.

At that time Félix was just entering his thirty-sixth year, by which time many are fathers, heads of family, and some, statesmen. He was merely an idle, unambitious fellow. His life had been a unique mixture of elegy and melodrama. He had spent the first years of his youth yearning for all things ephemeral, and when he seemed to have been forgotten by both God and man, an unexpected inheritance fell into his hands, lifting him from poverty. Only Providence holds the secret of how to stave off the dullness of such jaded theatrics.

Félix had acquired some familiarity with work, when it was unavoidable for his livelihood; but ever since he had obtained sufficient means for deliverance from concern for the morrow, he had relinquished himself body and soul to the serenity of repose. Nonetheless, let it be understood, it was not the repose of the apathetic, nor the vegetative existence of indolent souls. It was, if I may say so, a vigorous repose, composed of all sorts of elegant, intellectual occupations available to a man in his position.

I would not say he was handsome, in the broad sense of the word; but his features were correct, his presence agreeable. He was well turned out, with natural grace and refined elegance. His complexion was somewhat pale; his skin, taut and fine. His expression was placid and indifferent, poorly set off by his ordinarily cold countenance, not infrequently dead.

His character and spirit will become better known through reading these pages, by following our hero throughout the incidents of the quite artless story I am going to tell. His character is flawed, illogical and lacking consistency. He is a complex man, incoherent and capricious, in whom opposing elements meet, both refined qualities and irreconcilable failings.

There were two sides to him and, although they melded into one face, they were distinct—one natural and spontaneous, the other calculating and systematic. The two blended, thus it was difficult to discern and define them. Within such a man, made up of sincerity and affectation, everything was confused and shuffled. A journalist at the time, a friend of his, used to compare him to the Shield of Achilles[3]—a medley of tin and gold—"much less solid," he would add.

Our hero had chosen that day, the dawn of the year, to have the sun set on his old love affair. Yet, the affair was not so old, just six months. Nonetheless, it was to end with no sense of loss or pity, not only because it had become burdensome, but also because Félix had just read a book by Henri Murger,[4] in which he had discovered a character prone to impetuous catastrophe. The woman of his thoughts, as a poet would say, thus received a coup, both moral and literary.

A half an hour after the doctor had left his position by the window, a visitor arrived, a forty-year-old man, in refined clothes, whose manners were at once familiar and grave, brash and discreet.

— Come in, Mr. Viana, said Félix when he saw him at the parlor door. You've come to join me for luncheon, I knew it!

— That's one of three reasons I've come, answered
Viana. But, I assure you, it's the last of them.

— What's the first?

— The first, said the newly arrived guest, is to wish you
the best for a happy new year. I rejoice in thinking this one
will transpire as well for you as did the last. The second
reason is to deliver a letter to you from the colonel.[5]

Viana removed a letter from his pocket and handed it
to the doctor, who read it quickly.

— Is it an invitation to a gathering this evening? Viana
asked when he saw him fold the letter.

— Yes. I'm put out, though, because I was planning to
go to Tijuca.[6]

— Don't give in to that, Viana answered. I think I'd
forego all the trips in the world so as not to miss one evening at the colonel's. He's a fine man and hosts wonderful
parties. Are you attending?

Félix hesitated at length.

— Look here, I've come charged with dismantling each
and every one of your objections, said Viana.

— I have none. The invitation upsets my plans; but in
spite of that, I'll accept.

— As well you should!

A house servant[7] came to say luncheon was served.
Viana removed his gloves and followed his host.

— What's new? Félix asked, seating himself at the table.

— Nothing I'm aware of, Viana answered, imitating his
host. Rio de Janeiro is going from bad to worse.

— Yes?

— It's true. There aren't even any scandals. We're living
in complete abstinence. The reign of virtue is upon us. You
see I, for one, am nostalgic for immorality.

Viana was essentially a quiet man with the need to appear libertine, resulting from the company he kept with several young men. Chaste by principle and temperament, he had the spirit of a libertine, but not the actions. He chastised those of dubious reputation, yet yearned for one his own. Moreover, he would have been secretly pleased to be named the subject of some amorous misdeed, and would have been decidedly negligent in defending his innocence, a contradiction that may seem absurd, but which was natural.

Since Félix had not risen to the realm of conversation Viana had proposed, the latter took to complimenting the wines.

— My gracious host, wherever did you find such good wines? he asked after finishing off a glass.

— In my pocket.

— You're right. Money buys everything, including good wines.

Félix answered with an ambiguous smile, which might have been either benevolent or malevolent, but seemed not to make any impression on his guest. Viana was a consummate parasite, whose stomach held greater capacity than his prejudice, a man with less sensitivity than disposition. Let it not be assumed, though, that poverty had led to this line of work. He had some inheritance from his mother, which he kept religiously intact, having lived until then off the income of a position from which he had recently resigned over a disagreement with his superior. Still, these contrasts between fate and character are not rare. Viana was merely a case in point. He was born a parasite as others are born dwarves. A parasite by divine right.

It does not seem likely to me that he had read *Sá de*

Miranda.[8] Nonetheless, he put into practice one of the poet's characters' maxims: "good looks, a good hat and good words, cost little and are worth a lot . . ."

In calling him a parasite, my allusion is not limited to his gastronomical vocation in the homes of others. Viana was also a parasite on kindness and friendship, the polished and cheerful intruder who, through art and persistence, managed to ingratiate himself where he had initially been received with tedium and indifference. He was one of those prying, pliable men who go everywhere and know everyone, "good looks, a good hat, and good words."

Since Félix was seemingly worried, Viana resolved not to say a word, awaiting the perfect opportunity. The coffee was served, and the doctor was the first to break the silence. Viana adroitly took up the thread of his compliments, which Félix had previously brushed aside so brusquely. This time Viana did not praise the wine, rather his host's personal traits, insisting that no one was more loved at the home of Colonel Morais, and that he himself could think of no one in the world the colonel held in higher esteem.

— You're so fortunate in this respect, Viana concluded, even people who've not seen you in a long while, wholly maintain the affection you've inspired in them. Can you guess whom I'm talking about?

— No.

— Well, you'll find out tonight, a person who admires you and hasn't seen you for a long time is coming to the colonel's house. Let's be frank, it's my sister Lívia.

— That surprises me, because I've only seen her twice.

— That's not possible, Viana insisted. I remember I

introduced the two of you myself. If I'm not mistaken, it was two years ago, on *Dia da Glória*.[9]

— I was coming down the hill, Félix continued, when I met you both. We stopped for five minutes or so. Then, that night we saw each other again at a ball. We greeted each other, no more than that.

— And that's all?

— Nothing more.

— In that case, concluded Viana, I think you hold the secret of how to enchant young ladies in a mere five minutes of conversation, plus a parlor greeting. My sister speaks of you often, at least since she's returned from Minas[10] . . .

— Ah! She was in Minas?

— She went nearly two years ago, after her husband died. She came back eight days ago. Can you imagine what she's proposed?

— No.

— A trip to Europe.

— And you're going?

— Lívia's wishes are my commands. Although, it may be better for me to go by myself. After all, a lady's always an obstacle for the immoderations of a sinner like myself. Don't you agree?

— So it's a journey for pleasure? Félix asked.

— Or romance. Lívia has this major flaw, she's a romantic. Her head's filled with intrigue, the natural fruit of the solitude she's lived these past two years, as well as the books she must have read. It's a shame, she's a good soul.

— I see she has all the necessary elements of a poet, the doctor observed. I recall she was pretty.

— Oh! In that respect, her widowhood has been a rebirth. She was beautiful when you saw her. Now she's fascinating. There are times I regret I'm her brother; I want to get down on my knees and worship her. Frankly, it's frightening.

Félix's lips barely traced a smile. Meanwhile, Viana proceeded with the panegyric of his sister, with enthusiasm at once sincere and partial. After a quarter of an hour he got up to leave.

— Until tonight? he said, shaking his host's hand.

— Until tonight.

Félix was alone.

"What kind of woman would she be," he asked himself, "beautiful enough to cause fear, amazing enough to cause regret?"

II

Liquidating the Old Year

A half an hour later, Félix stepped out of a tilbury[11] at the door of a house in Rocio.[12] He climbed the stairs slowly to the back door, left ajar. He strode through the house to the parlor, where his entrance went unnoticed by the young woman seated by the window, looking out over the street.

— Cecília! he said.

The startled young woman turned around.

— Ah! It's you. So late!

Felix approached her, kissed her, and took the book from her hand.

— Late? he said, leafing through the book. I couldn't have come earlier, I had visitors at home.

The young woman, pleased with his answer, stood up, putting her arms around his neck, asking:

— Are you dining with anyone tonight?

— I'm dining at home.

— At home? she repeated, and why not here?

— I can't.

— Do you have guests?

— No.

— You're dining alone?

— I'm dining alone.

— You prefer not to have my company? the young woman finally murmured in a sad voice.

— Cecília, Félix responded, lending his voice sweetness equal to the sternness of his resolution, there are circumstances that oblige me not to dine here today, nor ever.

Cecília went pale. Félix tried to reassure her, saying he would explain himself. Impervious to his words, she removed herself to the settee, remaining there in silence for a few moments. Félix paced the room, smelled the flowers placed in a vase that very day, perhaps to better receive him. He lit a cigar and went to sit opposite Cecília. The young woman stared at him, her eyes brimming. Then, as if her lips feared releasing a calamitous burst of some inner flame, she murmured these words:

— And why not ever more?

— Cecília, said the doctor, tossing away his freshly lit cigar, it's my misfortune that I can't understand happiness. My heart is flawed; my spirit, marred. My soul is dull, incapable of happiness, incapable of constancy. Love for me is an idyllic interlude, a short episode with neither flames nor tears. We've loved each other for six months. Why not start this New Year's Day afresh, and also start out a new life?

Cecília did not answer. She stared into his eyes which, if they were tender and lively in moments of joy, were then somber and grave. Félix took her hand. It was cold.

— Don't be dismayed. This isn't news to you, you've heard me say many times our affection is but a short chapter. You laughed at me then. You were mistaken, because you nurtured vain hopes.

— I was, Cecília interrupted, in a trembling voice. I see that now. It's true, I hoped with my constancy I'd be able to mend my ways, the errors weighing on my conscious. I clung to you as if to a life raft. But that raft didn't understand it was saving a life, and now it allows itself to be carried off by a wave, which is dragging it from my hands. I was mistaken. I don't blame you, I only hope you will do me justice . . .

— I will do you every justice, he replied, even as I admit I'm lacking in the qualities requisite for a redeemer.

Cecília was indifferent to his ironic tone. She didn not even hear him. She stood up, paced a bit. Then, leaning over the piano, her head between her hands, she sobbed at will. But this nearly silent outburst was short-lived.

A half an hour later Félix was taking leave of Cecília, all the while insisting he was departing like a gentleman, and that she would be receiving the necessary means to live by until she had forgotten him completely.

Cecília refused this act of generosity. Her firm disinterest surprised him greatly. He concluded she must have been harboring some amorous prospect.

He left.

On Rua do Ouvidor[13] he met Doctor Meneses, a young lawyer with whom he was acquainted.

— Come dine with me, he said.

— Aren't you dining with Cecília?

— I've finished with that chapter, Cecília's disengaged.

— Were there tears?

— Tears are part of the rite of separation. It was

unavoidable. Cecília shed a few tears, which I attempted to dry, promising her means for the foreseeable future. She refused, but I don't accept her refusal.

— You did wrong by separating from her, Cecília loved you.

— Meneses, said Félix, I'm never mistaken when I break a chain: I free myself.

— Perhaps you're right . . .

— But come dine with me, continued Félix, extending his arm.

— I can't, I'm going to dine with my mother.

— Ah!

— It's just two o'clock. I'll walk with you until three. Or are you going home?

— No.

They walked down the street arm in arm.

— If it's not indiscreet, Félix, said Meneses after a few minutes, was there a serious quarrel between you?

— No.

— Do you distrust her?

— Nor is that the case.

— So there was no quarrel, nor distrust. I know how fond she was of you, and you yourself have told me she was worth it. There were, therefore, millions of reasons for the two of you to proceed with the romance. Could it be that you have some marriage in view?

Félix laughed and shrugged his shoulders.

— Then I don't understand it, Meneses concluded.

— I'll tell you, responded Félix, my loves follow a system of semesters. They last longer than roses, two seasons. For my heart, a year is an eternity. No tenderness outlasts six months. At the end of that period, love packs its bags and leaves the heart like a traveler leaves a hotel . . . enter bother—a poor guest.

Meneses listened to Félix, his eyes cast downward. He barely smiled as Félix finished.

— Do you want to hear something? He asked.

— Proceed.

— Your cynicism seems hypocritical to me.

— It's neither cynicism nor hypocrisy, it's temperament.

— I don't believe so.

— Why not?

Meneses did not answer.

— I nearly regret our friendship, he said after some time.

— Aren't you my friend? asked Félix, with a mocking air.

Meneses stopped and confronted his companion.

— You doubt it?

— I don't doubt, but I'd ignored it till now. You recall our relations are relatively recent.

— What's the importance of time? There are friends made in eight days, while some remain indifferent after eight years.

— That's so.

The conversation took a turn. Meneses still attempted to talk about the young woman, but Félix paid him no attention. At three o'clock they separated, Félix to Laranjeiras, Meneses to Rocio.

Meneses was a good soul, compassionate and generous. All the illusions of youth were still in full bloom. He was enthusiastic and sincere, entirely lacking the slightest hint of calculation. With the passing years, it is possible he would come to lose some of his natural qualities, for not everyone can resist the two terrible solvents of time: acts of fortune and attrition of character. But, as of then, it was not yet the case. Cecília's situation had moved him. He decided to go to her.

Cecília was resigned, but saddened. When Meneses entered the room, she was at the piano, her head resting on one of her hands, her fingers running over the keys. She told him everything that had transpired, confessing that Félix's sudden change of heart had come as a shock. She said she was in great pain and would give anything to relive the recent past, but that she nurtured no hope of reconciliation.

— And if I try to do something?

— You'll try in vain, she answered. Besides which, I have no right to prolong happiness incompatible with his will. I was mistaken, trusted too much. I'd be mistaken to hold out any hope . . .

— Who knows, Cecília? said the young man, putting his hand on her shoulder, it's possible Félix gave in to a whim. He'll regret it eventually, but his pride will prevent him from taking the first step. In that case an influential person could convince him that the first glory is to make amends.

Cecília shrugged her shoulders, the extent of her response.

Meneses asked if there might be any cause for jealousy.

— I can swear to you, during this entire time I belonged to him exclusively.

Cecília's avowal would have meant very little seen

through the eyes of a man fully aware of the gamut of resources available to a woman of her circumstances. But Meneses was innocent in such matters. He left there feeling only pity. That same afternoon he sent a letter to Laranjeiras, precisely when Félix had just read another letter, from Cecília. The young woman's letter was calm, almost noble. She neither recriminated him, nor begged for any favors. She merely defended herself, recanting any responsibility for the separation.

Meneses's letter was gentlemanly. Therein he revealed the state of Cecília's soul and did not neglect mentioning the *Dardanian fugitive's*[14] lack of gratitude. Félix smiled as he read both missives, then threw them into the waste and never saw them again.

III

To the Sound of the Waltz

The colonel's house could have accommodated thrice the number of people invited for that evening's soirée, but the colonel preferred to include only relatives and his closest friends. He was a man of simple tastes who appreciated intimacy, above all.

When Félix arrived they were dancing a quadrille. The colonel approached him in greeting and led him to his wife, who was already awaiting him anxiously. The reason being, she said, was that he was one of the few young men willing to converse with elderly women, while in the presence of young ladies. Félix sat down next to Dona Matilde.[15] He was in good spirits and conversed in pleasantries until the music stopped.

The colonel's wife was of a motherly nature. She was forty years old, yet her features maintained the rose of youth, albeit somewhat wilted. They held a mixture of austerity and warmth, extreme generosity and extreme rigidity. She adored conversation and laughter, and was unusually fond of argument, except regarding two points, which to her mind were above human controversy: religion and husbands. Her greatest hope, she insisted, would be to die in the arms of both. Occasionally Félix reminded her it was not right to judge by appearances, and that the colonel, husband of excellent repute, was in fact an impenitent sinner. The good lady would laugh at these futile efforts to dislodge her husband's good name. A wondrous peace reigned over that couple, who had known how to substitute the flames of passion with the reciprocity of confidence and respect.

The conversation with the hostess was stealing some of Félix's time away from the young ladies, according to the expression on the colonel's face. He should divide himself with the ladies who still maintained some love of choreographic exercise. He refused, on the pretext of Dona Matilde's presence.

— Oh! Not on my account! responded the good woman. An elderly lady's rights are curbed by those of the young. Go on, doctor, and come back to me later, if they don't latch on to you elsewhere.

There was a waltz. Félix stood up and went in search of a partner. Having no preference among any of the ladies, he reminded himself to invite the colonel's daughter. He was crossing the parlor to meet her face to face when a waltzing couple collided into him. Even though he had practice navigating those waters, he was unable to avoid the whirl. He maintained his balance with rare fortune and sought out the best route, edging his way along the wall. At that moment, the waltzers stopped nearby. He thought he recognized Lívia, Viana's sister. With her cheeks flushed and palpitating breast, the young lady rested her arm softly on her partner's. She murmured a few words Félix could not make out and, after glancing around, continued waltzing.

This lasted minutes.

As soon as he was freed, Félix sought out the colonel's daughter, an interesting child of seventeen,[16] of slender figure, angelic face, and graceful forms, all languid and fragrant. She was one of those women reminiscent of a fine porcelain vase, one touches them with fear of breakage. Raquel was her name. She had great pretensions of being a woman, which were not unbecoming to her at that transitional age. Actually, Félix thought her childlike quality was precisely what suited her best. Her mother lavished her with praise, well founded though, in spite of its provenance.

Raquel accepted the invitation. Félix placed his arm around her waist, and she trembled from head to foot. Then she gave in to him with all the abandon a waltz requires or permits, and they flew around the salon in the general whirl. The agitation somewhat flushed the young woman's cheeks, normally without color. When they stopped she was breathless.

— Shall we sit? said Félix.

— No, let's stroll a little. Why don't you ever call on us?

— I'm in fear of finding no one at home. You're all always out . . .

— Not so! We've been in town for two months. Mother said this constant traveling doesn't agree with her, and I think she's right. It tires me, too. Father is the most enthusiastic.

— Don't you like country life?

— I have no preference, I like the country as much as the city. Even so . . . I fare better here. Are you looking at that young woman? Don't you find her pretty?

— Who? I wasn't looking at anyone.

— Well then, the loss is your own, because she's truly worth taking a look at. Lívia reigns tonight.

Even though Raquel, in Félix's opinion, was but a young woman, he could not help but notice how she so easily ceded the kingdom of the evening to the other woman. Yet, on the other hand, he reflected, the abdication may well have been affected modesty. Nonetheless, the young woman's clear gaze revealed absolute naiveté. He complimented her loveliness and set to admiring from afar that of Lívia.

Lívia did in fact have the air of a queen, a natural majesty, not conventional stiffness, but an involuntary grandiosity all her own. Félix's impression was at once good and bad. He found her astoundingly beautiful, but he sensed behind that regal face a soul both haughty and disdainful.

— She'll reign this evening, he said, turning to Raquel, but I won't be the one to court her.

— Why not?

— She seems proud, probably treats everyone as if they were her vassals. Don't you see how she listens disdainfully to her partner, who's offered her his arm?

The gentleman was the same young man who had waltzed with the widow, a Doctor Batista, a direct descendent of Camões' Leonardo,[17] "sentimental, and romantic."

— Oh! That's not the reason, said Raquel, Lívia doesn't like him.

A short time later, supper was served. Félix made his way toward an inner parlor, where the colonel kept his tomes, and which was temporarily serving as a refuge for smokers. Félix lit a cigar and began looking over the books. There were several other young men there, speaking enthusiastically about Viana's sister. She was the main attraction of the evening. And it was amidst the apologias of those courtiers of beauty that the young lady herself appeared on the colonel's arm, walking through the parlor toward the powder room.

— Doctor! said Viana, approaching Félix.

And turning to his sister:

— Doctor Félix wants to speak to you.

— Ah! said the young woman, glancing at the doctor.

Félix moved toward her.

— You don't remember me? he asked.

— Doctor Félix? But of course, although we were introduced quite some time ago, I have a good memory. What's more, only common people are forgotten.

Félix thanked her for the flattering remark. She held out her fingertips, elegantly clad in kid gloves. They exchanged a few more words. Shortly thereafter, having heard the prelude of a quadrille, everyone left. Félix and Moreirinha remained.

Moreirinha was about thirty years old, sporting a thick moustache, a pleasant bearing, and a frivolous spirit. He confessed he was impressed by the widow, but the rivals were too numerous.

— But are these rivals to be feared? Félix asked.

— No, only one of them.

— Which one?

— Batista.

— Is he in her good graces?

— I don't know, but he's the most valiant among them. Furthermore, he has the most time, even though he's married.

— Married?

— To an angel.

Félix tried to hearten the suitor, recalling all his deserving qualities. He invented some Moreirinha did not possess and reminded him of those he did, even if these were of relative or dubious worth. There was no doubting Moreirinha's reputation among the women. He was gallant by nature, as well as by design. In addition (and crucial), he held the unshakable conviction that his conversation was preferred among the ladies. No one knew better than he how to flatter the feminine *amour propre*. Nary a one dedicated more of his soul to the more delicate social graces, which on many occasions constituted a man's reputation. He put together picnics, purchased the most fashionable novels and musical scores, reserved boxes for celebrated performances, escorted pianists to soirées, and maintained such an accommodating manner withal that all the ladies carried a torch for him.

Félix returned to the salon as they were dancing the final steps of the quadrille. Lívia was splendidly graceful and elegant. Neither affected nor bashful, her movements were at once unencumbered and modest. The doctor tried to determine if the suitor was in the young woman's good graces, but he danced on the same side as she, thus their eyes could not meet. One of the colonel's nephews drew his attention to Batista's wife, a young woman of twenty, blond, rather pretty and worthy of inspiring love. To what end would the recently wed husband choose to burn in a foreign temple the incense his wife deserved?

Some time after the quadrille, Félix was inclined to leave the colonel's house, but the latter intercepted him, on the part of his wife and the young women. Félix explained he was indisposed.

— A dandy's excuse, said the old man, laughing mirthfully. I'm not going to allow you to leave, even if you drop dead on the parlor floor. If you please, my lady.

These last words were directed to Viana's sister, who was approaching the modest drawing room, where the two were conversing.

— Do you have a request for me, Colonel? she said, pausing.

— Only a favor. Retain this gentleman, who's bent on leaving us. I'm not up to it. See to it, for me. You can start by granting him a quadrille.

— I'll give him the next, which is my last.

— You're also on your way?

— Yes.

— Good Heavens, it's an exodus. I'll have the doors locked.

The colonel removed himself after this threat. Félix offered Lívia his arm and they went to sit on a nearby divan.

— My brother is very much your friend, said Lívia, accommodating the silken drapes of her dress. He often speaks to me about you.

— He's a good friend of mine, Félix repeated, grimacing to himself.

— It's no wonder, she observed, you deserve the esteem, sir.

— Why make such a claim?

— Everyone says it's so.

— Not everyone is sincere, Félix observed.

Félix harbored no illusions regarding Viana's esteem.

Without denying the widow's brother's friendship, he nonetheless considered it of limited worth. Lívia claimed, meanwhile, that her brother spoke of him with great enthusiasm, and to a certain extent, the enthusiasm was genuine. Félix held a certain moral ascendance over Viana; besides, Viana was a frank, generous man, coarse, but accommodating.

After a while, the conversation between the doctor and the widow began to lose the cold formality with which it had begun. They talked of the ball, and Lívia was expansively joyful in conveying her excellent impressions, especially, she said, because she had come from the countryside, where she had led a reclusive, monastic life. They spoke naturally of the trip she intended to take. She confessed it was a long-standing desire, postponed on numerous occasions.

— Don't think, Lívia added, that I'm only seduced by the splendors of Paris, or the elegance of European life. I have other wishes and ambitions. I want to see Italy and Germany, recall our own Guanabara Bay[18] while on the banks of the Arno and Rhine. Have you never had such yearnings?

— I would enjoy being able to, if all the bothers of travel could be done away with, but with my sedentary habits, the likelihood is slight. I participate in nature like plants do, by staying put. Your highness is more like the swallows . . .

— So I am, she said, reclining gently into the sofa, a little swallow, curious to see what lies beyond the horizon. An hour of pleasure is worth several days of tedium.

— It's not, answered Félix, smiling. The sensation of

that rapid instant is fleeting. The imagination may still guard a slight memory, but eventually everything dissipates in the dusk of time. Look, my two poles are Laranjeiras and Tijuca. I've never gone beyond these two extremes of my universe. While I confess to the monotony, I take pleasure in the very same.

Lívia took up the argument against what seemed to her a noteworthy paradox, although her words held not a trace of pedantry. She had a natural, plain manner of saying the least vulgar things in this world. She was able to express her ideas elegantly, yet without pretension.

The prelude to a waltz called their attention back to the ball. Félix invited her to waltz. She excused herself, saying she felt fatigued.

— I saw you waltzing when I came in, said Félix, I'm convinced very few can waltz as well as you. Believe in the sincerity of my compliment, for I never make them, ever.

The young lady accepted the compliment with ingenuous satisfaction.

— I like the waltz very much, she said. And it's no wonder, for it's the most important dance in the world.

— In any case, it's the only dance with poetry, added Félix. The quadrille has a certain geometric rigidity, but the waltz has all the abandon of the imagination.

— Exactly! Lívia exclaimed, as if Félix had gathered in a just few words her ideas on the subject.

— Furthermore, the doctor continued, encouraged by the widow's enthusiasm, the French quadrille is the very negation of dance, with the modern attire also the negation of grace, and both, sons of this century, the negation of everything.

— Oh! she murmured, smiling.

And the protest was not only with her lips, but with her eyes—eyes that were velvet and shining, made for the swooning of love. Félix began to feel comfortable next to that young woman and, gladly forgetting the party where he was apparently a mere fixture, he remained a long while there with her, oblivious to the comments of others, entirely given over to the fancy of his own thoughts.

Nonetheless in mid-conversation, he escaped—I'm not certain with which phrase of melancholic skepticism—leaving the young woman disquieted. Lívia looked at him, then to the floor, seemingly so absorbed she did not even notice the silence that ensued, following her gesture and Félix's words. He took advantage of the situation to examine her more fully.

Lívia appeared to be about twenty-four years old. She was extremely lovely, her beauty enhanced by her modest awareness of her graces, something similar to the tranquility of strength. Not one of her gestures revealed the self-absorption so commonly innate to beautiful women. She knew she was attractive, but believed if nature had been generous to her, it was to add to the harmony and order in earthly things. To exaggerate her graces seemed to her a crime; while to shirk their dignity, a frivolity.

Félix examined her at length, her head and her face, a model of ancient grace. Her complexion, slightly dark, had the softness perceived by the eyes before the touch of the hand. Her smooth, wide brow would seemingly never be troubled by reflection. Nevertheless, anyone examining the young woman's face at that instant would see she was no stranger to inner strife: her lively eyes had moments of languor. On that occasion they were neither alive nor languid. They were still.

It seemed as if she were looking with her spirit.

— Thank you, she murmured distractedly.

Afterwards, seemingly embarrassed by the long silence, she feigned nervous discomfiture. They stood up and moved toward the parlor. There, amidst the conversation and commotion, she regained her composure. They conversed at length, vivacious and attentive. The widow was slightly sarcastic, but it was benevolent, easy sarcasm, of the type that knowingly mixes thorns and roses. Félix knew her for the first time, even having seen her twice before, for it is not enough to see a woman to know her, it is necessary to hear her also; although oftentimes hearing her is enough to know her nevermore.

Lívia remained at the colonel's house for longer than she had promised, a miracle due to the doctor, according to Viana. There was one certainty, for the rest of the evening they virtually existed for no one but each other.

This did not go unperceived among several wagging tongues. One gentleman said to a lady:

— Does it not seem to you that Dona Lívia has deplorable taste?

With a slight upward movement of her the left side of her lips, the lady responded:

— That of Félix is no better.

The widow left amid a general murmur of curiosity. Félix did not remain at length thereafter. He thrust himself into his carriage and went to Laranjeiras.

Within one hour after the ball, the widow, the dance—everything—evaporated from his soul, thanks to his tranquil, peaceful slumber, like various random golden clouds nighttime either absorbs or disperses.

IV

Prelude

The following day Félix departed for Tijuca, where he maintained a residence for relaxation and refuge. He returned weeks later. Throughout his stay there, he knew nothing of the occurrences in town. He read neither the newspapers nor did he open correspondence from friends.

Something, nonetheless, had taken place. The first news with which he was greeted upon arriving back in the city was that Cecília had won over Moreirinha's heart.

Félix's successor, shortly after the arrival of the original suitor, lost nary a moment in sharing his good fortune. I know not whether for his foolishness or dramatic vengeance.

— May I congratulate you, Félix responded; you've taken on a calm, sweet young lady, capable of understanding you . . .

— So much the better! the young man rejoined. Precisely what I was in want of: a woman to understand me. Cecília is most definitely not a lost soul. She hasn't anything in common with other women on whom I've wasted my money with no more than a few belated regrets. She's a young lady of fine sentiment, maintaining a certain dignity in vice, a noble soul, elevated . . .

This panegyric lasted for several more minutes. In such a short time, had Moreirinha discovered qualities heretofore unknown to Félix? Would Moreirinha be more a fool or more perceptive? Cecília was certainly no hypocrite when it came to speaking of her fondness for a man. No matter the nature of her affections, she felt them sincerely. It was nonetheless unusual for the source of her affection to outlive four and twenty hours. Her constancy throughout the six months of her intimacy with Félix was undeniable. Yet, while she was a one-man sort of lover, she was also independent enough to forget him quickly. Her constancy was born of habit. Her maxim: never forget the present lover, recall the past lover, nor concern oneself with the future lover.

Moreirinha was her present lover. He could thus count on the young woman's devotion, or, at the very least, on her good intentions.

When Meneses learned of the dénouement he was stunned. His initial reasoning was that it was no more than one of Moreirinha's affectations, but he was soon disavowed of this conjecture. He sought out the doctor.

— My friend, he said, I beg your forgiveness for the ridiculous letter I wrote you.

— What letter?

— Regarding Cecília. I never believed those tears to be false, they went straight through my heart. I've learned to be less simplistic.

— You've learned no such thing, Félix retorted,

shrugging his shoulders. Sailors aren't made on land, but at sea, braving storms.

Cecília's amorous adventures were the topic of conversation among the young men's set. Before long, there was more to contemplate. With time, very few turned a blind eye to the petite brunette's afternoon carriage rides along Botafogo beach,[19] the altar at which Moreirinha would make his daily and pecuniary sacrifices. Initially, Félix was surprised at these habits, so contrary to Cecília's idle inclinations. Nonetheless, he soon divined the key to the enigma. Moreirinha could not fathom happiness without public admiration. For him, Kythera Island would never ever be that of Robinson Crusoe.[20]

In the meantime, a month had passed since the counselor's soirée.[21] Félix had not taken advantage of the invitation the widow had extended to him, nor ceded to Viana's insistence. However, one evening he chanced upon them at the theater. He was seated in the orchestra when he saw them in the loges. At the end of the second act, Félix approached their box.

He was graciously greeted, although the widow, without leaving off her courtesy and grace, seemed somewhat reserved and preoccupied. She did not speak with the same ease as she had on the evening at the ball. At times she forgot herself and those around her. On two occasions she answered a question that had not been posed and then neglected to answer one that had been.

The conversation, therefore, was not very lively. Fortunately Vianna took it upon himself to fill the intervals with the symphony of his thoughts. When the curtain was raised on the third act, Félix wanted to leave, but both the widow and her brother entreated him not to. He accepted their invitation. As to the performance on stage during that act, it most certainly left Félix unawares. The act was short, and Félix took advantage of the duration to observe the attitude of the young woman who, reclining languidly in her seat, was distractedly following the actors' dialogue.

"What could the young lady be thinking of?" Féliz said to himself. "Evidently, neither the sighs of the gallant leading man, nor the jesting of the farceur. She's watching the scene, but she doesn't see. Could she be awaiting some negligent lover? But who? Who's the imbecile who would allow such beautiful eyes to sadden?"

The play's ingénue who, since the previous act, was known to be passionately in love with the leading man— as occurs both in the theater and in the world—entered onstage precipitately, throwing herself into the arms of her loved one. This unexpected and vigorous resolve was awarded with tepid applause. And thus began a sentimental, passionate dialogue between the lady and the gallant leading man, a duel of sighs, declarations of devotion and constancy, to which the audience listened with great enthusiasm.

"She's in love, there's no doubt," Félix's musings continued, "it's enough to see her eyes shine with each line of the dialogue. She's pleased with the lover's protests and the lady's tears. I believe I've just smiled in approval. Oh! How divine she is!"

Finally, the curtain dropped. By the end of act three the widow had apparently reverted to her previous woes. She stood up, saying she must take her leave.

Viana beseeched her to remain till the end of the play.

Nonetheless, she insisted, and he had to give way. Félix accompanied them to the carriage.

— Till when? Lívia asked as she accepted Félix's extended hand.

— Soon.

Would it be serendipitous or illusory? Félix sensed strong pressure from the young woman's fingers as she climbed hurriedly into the carriage. His inclination was to respond in turn, with an even stronger clasp, but he was too late. The young woman was already settled, and Viana was about to step up into the carriage.

Illusion, certainly. Illusion or happenstance. But the doctor did not realize it straight away, and it was thus he first erred in his manner of judging the widow.

A few days after the encounter at the theater, Félix headed off to Catumbi,[22] where they lived. He did not find them. Lívia returned to the house and learned of Félix's visit when the servant girl[23] gave her his calling card. She removed her gloves so hastily they tore. When her brother commented as much, the young woman replied bitterly. Viana, accustomed to her crossness, shrugged his shoulders and took his leave.

Félix happened upon her two days later on the Rua do Ouvidor, as she was in the midst of shopping for her voyage.

— Had I known you were coming, I would not have left the house, said the widow.

Félix bowed.

— Although I enjoyed my outing. Living so far removed, I shan't expect to have the pleasure of receiving you a second time, I suppose it was better than nothing at all.

— The tilbury shortens distances, Félix observed. I'll seek to discharge the obligation I've incurred.

— That you've already accomplished. Now . . .

— Pardon me, but your compliment renews my obligation.

They parted ways.

Meneses, who was on the opposite side of the street during the few words exchanged between Félix and the widow, crossed over to greet his friend.

— Who is that young woman?

— Viana's sister.

— Bravo! She's stunning.

— She's truly beautiful, deserving of admiration far and wide. See how everyone has their eyes on her . . .

— With no indiscretion intended, said Meneses after watching her go into a shop, would you be burning your perfumes at that altar?

— No. To what end?

— Perhaps some marriage brewing . . .

— Marry . . . ? said Félix laughing. The question is so original, it deserves a sherbet. Let's go to the Carceler.[24]

At the Carceler, Meneses told Félix he had been distraught and saddened of late. He lived matrimonially with a pearl whom he had only recently retrieved from the mire. The previous day, he had discovered the traces of another admirer of precious gems at his home. He was certain of his lover's infidelity and sought Félix's counsel.

— No, I'm not lending you any advice, answered the doctor, you resolve it yourself.

— But, were I able to solve anything in the state I'm in, I wouldn't have come to talk to a friend.

— I'm flattered by your choice, but that is the extent of it. Imitate me if you can, but do not ask for my thoughts.

— But in my case, what would you do?

— Nothing at all. I'd take my hat and my leave.

— And if you were unable to do that painlessly.

— An absurd hypothesis.

— In your case.

— Naturally.

There was a pause.

— I'll give you some advice after all, said Félix.

Meneses looked up anxiously.

— No matter what you resolve, continued Félix, do not back away one step.

— And where am I to find this resolve?

— Here, said Félix, putting his finger to his head.

— Oh, no! Meneses sighed, the head has nothing to do with this. All the pain resides in my heart.

— Resort to surgery, cut it out by the root.

— How?

— Restrain your heart.

V

I'll Stay

Two days later, Félix was dressing for Catumbi when Meneses entered his home. He arrived pale and worn, with bloodshot eyes and a precarious gait. He did not sit down, rather, he plunged into a chair.

— What is this? Félix asked.

— It's all over, Meneses answered. The last of the links have fractured. It's cost me plenty, but it was unavoidable. It happened just now, I've come directly. I needed some-one with whom to vent. It's ridiculous, I well know it. But what's to be done? I suffer . . . with my miserable heart . . . allowing myself to be led by it . . .

Seemingly sympathetic to the young man's despair, Félix spoke some words of encouragement, which Meneses heard and acknowledged.

— I'd already suspected I'd been betrayed, said Meneses. But my conjectures were confirmed yesterday. What most causes me pain, withal—he continued after a few moments of silence—is that I came to the aid of the man who betrayed me, I'd attempted every kindness. And I'll be frank, I made him some loans.

— That's precisely why I never lend money to anyone, responded Félix, combing his sideburns.

— But how is one to suspect ill when faced with a smiling countenance? I trusted them both.

Félix shrugged.

— Have a cigar, he said.

— I don't want to smoke.

— Smoke! I've come to observe that smoke impedes the flow of tears, while carrying a sort of beneficial brume to the brain.

— Are you on your way out? asked Meneses, noting Félix was donning his hat.

— I'm going to Viana's house. Won't you accompany me?

— I cannot.

— But I insist, I could introduce you to his sister, then we'd spend several hours in pleasant company. You'd find yourself forgetting your sorrows directly.

Meneses refused. Félix then took him by carriage to his home on Rua do Lavradio.[25]

Along the way they discussed their vanished loves. Menses swore this was the last adventure to which he would expose his heart. He thought he was cured, for once and for all.

— Make no claims, Meneses, you may be mistaken. Do you know what you lack? Character. Tomorrow, between a few tears, a ray of sun will shine through and, low and behold, you'll be in love again, with all the confidence and risk that entails.

— Oh! No! Meneses protested.

— Would that you be right! But I'm here, and what I read in your expression is that the only way to save you from this shipwreck is to provide you with another ship. It will be far too late by the time you convince yourself that to live is not to obey passions. Instead, to live is to repulse or smother them. Mollycoddles like yourself cry. Men either don't feel or stifle what they do feel. There's no solution, my friend, is what I'd say, if I didn't recall your fortunate rival, who is a perfect rogue. Come along to Viana's house, you'll most certainly be fond of Lívia. You and she are alike.

— I can't, responded Meneses, who had only heard the last portion of Félix's words.

— But you'll come later?

— Yes, later.

— And you'll fall passionately in love with her?

Meneses smiled with melancholy. The carriage came to a halt and they took their leave of one another. Félix continued on to Catumbi, where he found Lívia alone at home. She had been invited to a dinner but had refused, on the pretext of some false ailment. Her brother took it upon himself to represent her.

— I had a premonition, she said after recounting this to the doctor, I had a premonition that you would come today and I did not want to repeat what happened the first time.

— And you believe in premonitions? asked Félix.

— I can't explain them, but I believe in them.

Lívia seemed more beautiful than on previous occasions. It was not only the natural lighting, complementing her complexion to advantage, but also the simplicity of her attire, heightening the effect of her person. Félix did not dissemble the impression the young woman's new appearance elicited. Lívia, like all beautiful women—given that she was not vain—knew how to see her own reflection in the faces of others. The doctor's impression did not go unnoticed.

Their leave-taking at the carriage had not left Félix's spirit. He had convinced himself of two things: first, the widow was fond of him; second, to win her over was elementary. All appearances bolstered his opinion that the young woman was in love with him. Félix seized the opportunity and set out to take every possible advantage. Nonetheless, that day he did not prolong his visit. When he announced he was leaving, the widow asked that he not forget to call on them.

— I'll use the time well, observed Félix, between now and your departure to Europe. Your brother told me the trip is upon you.

— If nothing upsets our plans. In any case, come, and don't make these doctors' calls.

— I was a doctor, I fell into that habit, answered Félix, smiling.

— You're no longer a doctor?

— For the body, no.

— And for the soul?

— Perhaps. I've just left someone whose soul is suffering, and whom I would like to introduce you to, because these airs are healthy, I believe.

— What ails your patient?

Félix smiled.

— The victim of inconstancy, a common disease. He's in the acute stages. He's an unfortunate young man, unassuming and innocent, who seeks the rules of life in textbooks, compendiums of the imagination. Bad books, don't you agree?

Lívia did not answer. She had grown dizzy listening to him.

— Meneses doesn't know any others, Félix continued. He's like the son of that ancient astrologer who, in contemplating the stars, fell into the abyss. I'm of the old opinion, which the astrologer expounds, "If you don't see what's at your feet, why question what's above your head?"

— The astrologer might answer, observed the widow, that eyes were made to contemplate the stars.

— He'd be correct, my lady, if he could eliminate the abyss. But what is life, if not a combination of stars and abyss, rapture and precipice? The best way to escape the precipice is to escape into rapture.

Lívia was pensive for a few seconds.

— That's a melancholy thought, she said, although it may be true. But why should we condemn those who lead a contemplative life when they know no other? Books for the imagination . . . they aren't detestable, as you have said, sir. They're neither detestable nor excellent. God gives them out according to each person's particular way of being.

Félix took his leave from Lívia, not enraptured, nor with throbbing heart, but ready for an adventure. He increased his visits to Catumbi, much to Viana's delight as he began to sense a growing affection between the two of them, perhaps a family alliance. Félix's presence was actually advantageous to the siblings' household. The widow and her brother were worlds apart, dissimilar in sentiment, in living habits, and in their manner of thinking. Lívia fluctuated between moments of affability and brusqueness, while her brother was of an unalterably peaceful nature. Viana had good and bad qualities, but the good were precisely those in opposition to the speculative nature of the widow. He was essentially a practical man, his kingdom was entirely of this world. In spite of his pretensions of brashness and extravagance, he was an orderly and economic young man. Lívia in this respect was negligent and "scatterbrained," as her brother referred to her. She often withdrew from her surroundings to reach a superior, chimerical world. The doctor was a sort of compliant mediator between them. He did not fit in to either of their spheres, but was dextrous in maintaining their rapprochement.

On a few occasions, Félix encountered Doctor Batista in Catumbi, whom he had seen dancing with the widow at the colonel's house. Lívia seemingly paid him no attention, nor did the intended take offense at this. He was a model of dissimulation and calculation. He knew all the artifices involved in the amorous crusade, the indifference, the disdain, the enthusiasm, and even the resignation.

One evening when they left together, Félix attempted to assess Doctor Batista's sentiment in relation to the young woman.

— There's nothing to it, responded Batista with indifference; nor do I intend to court her. However, were those my intentions, I would triumph. Patience is the master key to love.

— Don't you find your maxim immoral?

— In practice, life is such . . . but these loves are so delicious for this very reason.

Fifteen days later Viana appeared at Félix's house. He confided that his sister no longer had any intention of traveling to Europe.

— Why ever not? asked Félix.

— That's precisely what I wanted to know, he said with a gesture of barely contained disdain. But I'm certain I'll never find out. That sister of mine doesn't seem to have her faculties about her.

— There must be some reason. Could she be sick?

— She's in perfect health.

— Who knows . . . some romance? A beau?

— I've thought of that, it could be some romance, perhaps a beau.

— At her age, passions reign. It would be fruitless to try to dissuade her, and even if it weren't useless, it wouldn't be reasonable, because a young widow . . . she loved her husband very much, no?

— Prior to the marriage, very much, three months later, even more. By the time several months had gone by, she was neither here nor there. The whole story is a mystery to me . . .

— I see no mystery whatsoever. Marriage is precisely that. The effects settle, and thus become more lasting. If your sister's passion was tempered . . .

— That is not the circumstance. She didn't love any less, she found him boring . . . But why ponder these things we can't solve? The only explanation I have to offer is her strange nature. You, sir, have no idea of that young woman's endless variations in mood. Some days she gets

up sweet and happy, the next, she's entirely cross and melancholic. No-one understands her, and least of all me.

— Sir, mightn't you be exaggerating something that's
absolutely natural? We all have similar changes in humor.
Some mornings are happy, others, gloomy. Would you like
some advice? Never ever cross her, you'll fare better.

— But, sir, you must agree, once one has had a taste of
a Parisian life . . .

— There's a time for everything, said Félix, and you, sir,
are still young. We'll go together in a year's time.

— Your word?

— My word.

VI

Declaration

— So, you're no longer making your voyage to Europe?
Félix asked the widow that same afternoon.

— Who told you that?

— Your brother.

— I've cancelled the trip, truly against his wishes. He's
called me capricious and I don't know what else. He may
be right. At times even I don't understand myself. This
trip, which was such an ardent wish, now leaves me cold.
What do you think of that?

— There must be some reason, the doctor pondered,
and I would sense if the reason were . . .

— If the reason were? the young lady repeated.

They were silent for some time, looking at each other.
Their lips neither asked nor offered any explanation as they
pondered in wonder, reading each other's eyes.

Lívia lowered hers.

— Let's step out on the terrace, she said finally. It's a
lovely afternoon.

It was, in fact, a lovely afternoon. Félix, however,

thought less about the afternoon than he did about the young woman. He did not want to miss the occasion to tell her, as if it were true, that he was madly in love with her. Leaning over the balustrade and gazing out over the property, the widow feigned nonchalant contemplation. In reality, she was fine-tuning her listening, awaiting the amorous confession.

Félix looked at her, not daring to break the silence. Nearly bursting out with the decisive words, he asked himself, what if she were to weigh more into his future than he had imagined up to that time, and if a momentary lapse might not result in a lifetime of regret. But the hesitation was brief. Félix was finally on the verge of tempting fortune, when a servant appeared on the terrace to announce Doctor Batista's arrival.

— I don't want to speak with anyone at the moment, João, said the young lady. I'm indisposed.

— What kind of an answer is that? asked Félix, quietly, when the servant had turned to leave.

— João! said the young lady.

The servant returned.

— Today I can only receive our intimates, my brother's friends. Tell anyone else I am indisposed.

The servant left.

— Do you fancy the explanation?

— Well, it's probably for the best, Félix answered. Better for you, madam. Still, not on my behalf, I haven't intended to be included among the intimates of the household.

— Would you prefer I amend my orders . . . ?

— No, I wouldn't ask that of you. I don't have the right, nevertheless . . .

— And, nevertheless . . . ?

There was a brief silence.

— You don't take my meaning? said Félix, his voice barely audible.

— I do, she murmured, after a pause, but I'm afraid I may be mistaken.

— You're not mistaken, Félix insisted ardently. I love you, how could I ever deny it when my voice and expression have surely said it more clearly than my words. Haven't you realized this for some time? Couldn't you guess by now that for me, the hope of your love holds all the joy of tomorrow? Say so! Say just one word, cruel or kind, but a word, and let it be definitive.

Lívia listened to the doctor, enraptured, and her answer was more eloquent than his declaration. She offered him her hand, trembling and cold, and drank from his eyes a long look of gratitude and elation.

— You love me too? asked Félix after several minutes of silent reflection.

— Oh, very much! sighed the young lady.

And thus they remained in silence, breathless and in love, in the sweet ecstasy that is perhaps the greatest of the human soul. Both of them, because the doctor's heart, for that moment at least, was beating with equal fervor.

— Very much! Lívia repeated, as if these words were merely echoes of her feelings or an answer to the mute questioning from the doctor's eyes.

Félix put his arm around her waist and drew her tenderly to him. Then he held her head between his hands leaning down to kiss her forehead when a strange sound caused him to refrain, a childish, unfamiliar voice.

Seconds later on the terrace there appeared a boy of five years, a nice, clever child, flushed and plump, like the angels and cupids artists put in paintings.

— Mommy! Mommy! hollered the little one, running to embrace his mother and escape his nanny,[26] who came chasing after him.

Lívia took the child in her arms, kissed him and set him on her lap.

— May I introduce my son, she said to the doctor. He's just returned from his godmother's house.

And turning to the boy:

— Luís, you've met Doctor Félix?

The boy looked at the doctor with the stunned, inquisitive expression of children seeing someone for the first time. He then turned to his mother, seemingly not very impressed. Lívia covered his face with kisses. The child, laughing joyfully, pushed away that torrent of maternal caresses with his tiny hands.

— Well now, said the widow, who's permitted you to be scrambling about here?

— No one, the boy answered, I asked Clara to allow me to come, she didn't want to, but I came out just the same. Didn't I do right, mother?

— You did wrong. Go play, off with you, but no running.

— Who's that man? asked Luís, looking again at Félix.

— I've already told you, it's Doctor Félix.

— Ah!

Luís stared at the doctor, then looked at his mother, and indicated he wanted to get down. Lívia set him on the floor.

— May I go out to the fields?

— Yes, you may. Take him, Clara.

Luís ran away, followed by his nanny. His mother followed him with her eyes until he disappeared from the terrace.

During this scene, Félix seemed wholly perplexed by everything taking place around him. He did not hear the young woman's scolding, nor the child's babbling. He only heard himself. He contemplated the scene with envious delight, and felt a pang of regret.

"She's a mother," the young man said to himself, "she's a mother!"

— Look, the young woman was saying, leaning over the balustrade, which looked out over the fields, look how he scampers away . . .

Félix leaned over too. In fact, the boy was running ahead of Clara, who lagged far behind. Every once in a while, he would stop to wait for his nanny, but no sooner did she catch up with him, than he would teasingly set out running again. The mother seemed to have forgotten everything else. Félix contemplated her with religious respect. They remained in silence thus for several seconds. Suddenly Lívia turned to the doctor:

— See? she said, my happiness depends on very little: you, sir, and that child.

So saying, she tilted her head. Félix kissed her ardently, but could not say anything. Emotion blocked his voice; his reflections imposed silence.

VII

The Hawk and the Dove

Having boldly initiated the adventure, it was only natural that Félix left Catumbi filled with the vainglorious satisfaction of the victorious. Was he not loved, and loved through no effort of his own, without resistance nor combat? And the woman to whom he had so recently and frankly given his heart, did she not have all the qualities to seduce a man and flatter his vanity?

For anyone else this would have sufficed to provide a pervading sense of superiority in relation to all other mortals, yet the nature of the victory troubled Félix's happiness. To which end had his heart intervened in this episode, meant to be short lived, beautiful, with neither past nor future, ecstasy nor tears?

"I've gone too far," he was saying to himself. "I shouldn't encourage her passion or arouse her hopes, hopes culminating in nothing more than sorrow. What do I have to offer, how could I possibly correspond with her love? With my spirit, perhaps, my dedication, my tenderness, that's all . . . because love . . . I, in love? To place my entire existence into the hands of an unknown being . . . and more than my existence, my destiny? Unfathomable."

At this point, it seemed as if some sort of vague, remote idea surfaced in his soul and made a long excursion through the field of his memory. When he returned to the present, the carriage had entered the Largo de Machado. He descended and went home on foot.

The widow had begun to occupy his soul. Hence, he recapitulated everything that had taken place at Catumbi, the words exchanged, their tender gazes, their mutual confession. He conjured up the young woman's image, visualizing her close to him, tilting towards his lips, her heart throbbing with sentiment and tenderness. Thus this fantasy began to draft a future in his mind, neither marvelous nor legal; but real and prosaic, as he supposed was ordained for a man incapable of spiritual affections.

"And what else does she want?" said the doctor to himself. "It would have been, without a doubt, better had there been less sentiment in that declaration, had we sailed more closely to shore, instead of launching ourselves out to the high seas of the imagination. Well, after all, it's merely a question of form. Surely she feels as I do. Doubtless she's perceived it. Although it's true, she spoke with great passion. Still, naturally she knows her art, she's a colorist. Otherwise, it would have seemed as if she'd delivered herself out of curiosity, perhaps out of habit. A mad passion may justify a mistake. She's bracing herself for a mistake. Hasn't she been seducing me for some time? It's certain, it's right before my eyes. And I had imagined that . . ."

By the time Félix arrived home, he was entirely convinced the widow's affection was a mixture of vanity, caprice, and sensual inclination. This seemed more likely to him than disinterested, sincere passion, which, in any event, he did not believe in. It is no wonder then that, once again, thoughts of Lívia did not make their way into his slumber, and as dawn's first light eased through the bedroom windowpanes, falling upon the doctor's face, it was as grave and placid as the previous day.

Félix returned to Catumbi that very day. The widow was radiant with happiness, quivering with joy. She offered him her hand, which he pressed—it was not trembling like she was, but soft and graceful. Viana's presence, moreover, prevented any further show of affection. The parasite, who seemed set on establishing a family alliance with the doctor, was not inclined to be cruel to the two lovers. He thus shut his eyes and closed his ears and, if his presence was nonetheless inconvenient, it was not a case of will, rather of circumstance, because in these situations not even the entirety of Voltaire's wit can render a man interesting.

Félix visited with ever greater frequency, where on occasion, he met members of Colonel Morais's family, and on others, less frequent, Lívia's intimates. Dona Matilde was enthusiastic over the doctor. As for Raquel, she gazed at him with something like adoration. Among the men, some detested him cordially, others feared him, not a few envied him, and only a handful liked him.

Félix, meanwhile, seemed indifferent to the sentiments he inspired, and thus obeyed a system more or less compatible with his natural disposition. It was precisely that of his method in matters of love. Whenever possible, he refrained from advancing the young woman's hopeful confidence. Given that he was versed in the rhetoric of passion to its very depths, his shunning of its use, except with great parsimony, seemed to him a reasonable economy.

Lívia, however, neither dissembled nor hesitated. She allowed her heartfelt emotions to permeate her countenance. She played all her cards on the table with neither forethought nor calculation. Unreserved and discreet, lively and delicate, enthusiastic and thoughtful, Lívia possessed these apparent contrasts, which were no more nor less than the harmony of her character. Her very detractions were born of her qualities. She was gullible for her trusting nature, severe with all that seemed to her base or futile. Her imagination was chimerical, at times—her heart superstitious, her intelligence, austere, but she made up for all of these imperfections, if they were to be so considered, with her qualities both original and rare.

One day, when they were both conversing on the only topic that could possibly interest them—at least the one that interested her, Félix asked her to explain something that had evaded him, seemingly obscure.

— Obscure? repeated Lívia.

— Do you recall that night I met you at the theater? said the doctor. You were worried and oblivious to your surroundings. You conversed poorly and were distracted, interested in the romantic scenes, everything else seemed to bore you. At the end of the third act, you got up and left. You tell me, nonetheless, that ever since the colonel's soirée you'd already begun to feel this love, this love of your life. Well then, was I not there, next to you at the theater?

— No.

— Oh!

— That was another man, very different from the one

I see now right before me, because you didn't love me yet. But it wasn't only that; there was more. Do you think your actions, sentiments, and person, aren't the object of strangers' talk?

— I couldn't be less interested in talk!

— Well then, they spoke very badly of your heart that day.

— What did they say about this obscure wanderer?

— Wanderer?

— Former, Félix corrected himself.

— They told me a lot of bad things.

— Did you believe them?

— No, but I was aggrieved. I'd grown used to admiring you from afar. I knew you little, but my brother mentioned you often in his letters to me when I was in Minas, and Raquel's echoed his.

— Your brother is somewhat enthusiastic about me, said Félix. So, naturally he exaggerates my qualities. As for the colonel's daughter, she's a child, who has grown accustomed to seeing me with the eyes of a little sister.

— So, you'd rather I believe the negative comments?

— Neither the bad nor the good, Lívia. Know me first, then you'll judge with certainty.

— Oh! But I do know you! she exclaimed.

Viana's entrance interrupted their talk. Félix went toward the table and opened an autograph book,[27] while Viana told his sister about the affairs at a dinner he had attended.

The widow's autograph book, which the doctor opened for the first time, was already filled with prose and verse. Not all of it was good, as is common with this literary form, at times the veritable asylum of Parnassian invalids where feeble rheumatic muses reveal their lamentations.[28] One page in particular seemed mysterious to him, it was an unsigned declaration of love. He read it, barely containing his smile, the only aspect worse than the form was the sentiment.

— What are you laughing at? asked the widow.

Viana approached Félix, glancing down at the open page.

— Ah! he said indifferently, that's by my deceased brother-in-law.

Lívia shivered and her color rose.

"The widow of a numbskull!" thought Félix. "She's in need of an intelligent man."

VIII

Fall

The outcome of this situation of inequality, a cold man and a woman who is passionately in love, would seem to be the woman's undoing. It was his. To make his conquest, Félix thought only of the results, whereas the widow—apart from her love—had two active, latent attendants working on her behalf: time and habit. Each passing day fell like a drop of water delving into the doctor's heart, carving deeply therein with the cold tenacity of destiny.

The reader will say ironic happenstance determined the outcome of circumstances that had appeared to be so distinct only a few weeks prior. Then best call it the logic of nature, for Félix's heart, apparently made of marble, was revealed to be made of no more than our common clay. It was surely not a virginal, pure heart. It contained that precise dose of egoism nature divvies out maternally to all men. Nor can it be said he was lacking in skepticism. Still, he exaggerated his shortcomings to the point where, in the view of others, they lost their original contours.

His swords were certainly made of fine metal, but if

they were good for fencing, they were of little value in a
sword fight. Had the young woman displayed just enough
affection to dissemble her error, our hero would have been
up to his reputation. But the widow's love was a veritable
battle. By the time Félix reached the point of confronting
her heart, he was entirely caught up in his fascination with
the abyss, and therein he fell.

His downfall, as I said, was slow. The doctor began
to feel the need for the young woman's presence. He felt
her long absences sorely, and, what was more, these were
assuaged by a sense of longing, which he defined differently, but which was, after all, longing. When he went to
call on her, as he drew closer towards her, he felt something beating inside his chest. He told himself it was his
blood, still young and restive. It could be a physiological
reason, but there was also a moral reason. It was the lava
of a passion forming and rising up into the throat of the
volcano. Long was the gestation of that love. By the time
the doctor discovered the state of his soul, the spark was
not to be extinguished, rather it had become a rampant,
all-consuming blaze.

In this case, let scholars decide which of these two loves
is better, the love that comes at full gallop, or that which
invades the heart at walking pace. I cannot decide; they
are both loves, both have their energies. Félix's seems to
have grown invincibly strong, in silence.

When man applies the bit for the first time on a frisky,
wild colt, that young steed is no less irritated than was our
hero on the day he felt the freedom of his heart violated.
Unusual and unfounded fury, yet bitter and sincere. Right
off he planned a violent separation, which would give him

the time and weaponry to win the battle against himself.
The execution of the plan followed the idea closely. The
doctor suddenly ceased his visits to Catumbi.

However, his absence was favorable to the widow's position. The doctor's vexation was not appeased, rather transformed; it no longer bore witness to his heart's weakness,
rather to its rebellion. That which had initially seemed
imperative to the restoration of his peace of mind began
in his eyes to take on the quality of ingratitude. Ingratitude
was to acknowledge a great deal, but the doctor went
beyond, he found himself ridiculous. By now, resistance
was no longer possible. Some men are able to find glory in
their own ingratitude, claiming with skeptical morality that
it is their road to independence. But no one is convinced of
their own ridicule; to be ridiculous demands a correction.

Beyond these justifications, the daughters of his conscience, there were others the doctor did not articulate, but
felt—the longings, the memories, the desire, the mysterious and constant voice whispering in his ear the name
Lívia.

Furthermore, the beautiful widow wrote him. Like a
true lover, Félix swore he would not open any letters she
might send him, then ran to the door to receive the first. It
was not a letter of recrimination, rather filled with surprise
and tears. When the second letter came, the doctor already
knew the first by heart. The second would be the last, she
wrote. The recriminations had begun, but not against him,
nor against destiny. They were recriminations against herself. The young woman's melancholic resignation moved
him. By the time the week was out, he was at her feet in
an act of sincere contrition.

Lívia forgave him the tears shed during the eight days of anxious uncertainty. She forgave him as truly good souls are able to—without resentment. But the cause of the absence remained unexplained by Félix.

— Haven't you already forgiven me? said the doctor, when she asked him directly. That's enough, don't try to learn the reason for this singular madness, which took me so far from the only place possible where I can feel happiness. For my atonement, the eight days I too have suffered is enough, plus the shame of having . . .

He held himself in check, feared saying everything. The young woman heard those words with frank satisfaction and murmured:

— Jealousy?

Félix shuddered, his eyes slightly clouding over. Lívia leaned toward him as if attempting to read in his countenance the truth he was endeavoring to hide.

— No, said Félix, it wasn't jealousy. Jealous of what and over whom?

— Over no one, I'm sure. Still, it seems to me your love is somewhat idealist, unsettled. Oh! I won't complain over such a trifle. I'd go so far as to thank you. What might I have lost? A few days of peace, perhaps—but the certainty of being loved makes it all worthwhile. Isn't purgatory the doorway to Heaven? Everyone loves in their own manner. The manner itself matters little, what is essential is knowing how to love. I may be mistaken, she continued, placing her hands on his head, but I believe you have an excessive imagination inside here, perhaps sickly. Or else . . .

— Or else? the doctor repeated, noting her pause.

— Or else the ailment is here, Lívia concluded, pointing

to his heart. It doesn't matter. I can withstand anything, as long as you love me.

— Oh! Lívia, exclaimed Félix, after kissing her forehead tenderly, your vow is the promise of our future. Look to your heart, see if you find enough forgiveness there, and I swear to you we'll be happy.

— I'll forgive anything, as long as you love me, the young woman said.

Would she have understood the painful, onerous obligation she was undertaking? Perhaps not. She trusted herself, the strength of her own love and that of Félix to overcome everything, to achieve what had become her life's dream.

The best route to this was certainly towards the church. What obstacle could there be? They depended on each other exclusively. Marriage was the logical and customary outcome of such a romance. But neither did the widow insinuate it, nor did the doctor suggest it and, in this poorly defined situation, several days passed in peaceful joy.

From the eyes of strangers, both sought to hide their secret. While Lívia's reserve was just enough to observe mores, Félix's was so complete and calculating the young woman herself was confounded. This effortless dissimulation disturbed her peace of mind. She thought it overly perfect. His apparent composure stood in contradiction to his impetuous love. Furthermore, why hide something so mysteriously that was, sooner or later, to become public knowledge?

Félix's indifference, meanwhile, was not as complete as it appeared to be, it was actually a heedful indifference.

When the widow's eyes sought out the doctor's, the latter would cautiously avert his; but then he would look, shall we say, from beneath his lids.

And thus began, for her, a life of struggle.

IX

Struggle

Félix's love had a bitter taste, ridden with doubt and suspicion. Testy, she had called him, and not without reason. He was wounded at the slightest brush of a rose leaf. A smile, a look, a gesture, anything was enough to perturb his spirit. The young woman's very thoughts were subject to his suspicions. If at any given moment he discovered thoughtful languor in her gaze, he would begin to speculate her reasons, recalling a gesture from the previous day, a poorly explained look, or some obscure, ambiguous sentence. It all blended together in the poor lover's soul. From all of this was born, authentically and luminously, the young woman's treachery.

Lívia certainly would have preferred honest, constant trust, but his suspicions far from embittered her heart; she accepted them joyously.

— Better this, she told him after a reconciliation, because I realize you love me. Trust can also be a sort of indifference, and indifference is the worst of all evils.

This philosophy led to occasional moments of dismay.

The strength of their love alone was not enough to forbear the daily suspicion, which sometimes faded quickly, but was renewed, only to fade and be renewed yet again. Lívia began to avoid places she had previously frequented. Rarely did she appear at the theater or at gatherings. Félix understood the reasoning behind her reserve and brought it to her attention. The young woman denied it. But, upon his insistence along this line of reasoning, requesting she not alter her habits, she answered:

— Be frank, Félix, we'll get on better. When I'm out, just like when I'm home—actually, out there is worse than here—the slightest incident is enough to put you out of spirits.

— I promise that's not true.

He would promise, then break his promise. His spirit could not ratify the promises his heart put forth.

To what end her enormous prudence in her relations with others, if it was all too little to gain Félix's trust? One hour of inalterable joy was bought at the cost of several hours of boredom and, on occasion, tears. He was certainly moved, and would make it up to her with sacrifices, if necessary. Nonetheless, these lucid moments were short lived.

At the outset, Lívia was not yet accustomed to reading the doctor's face. He had an extraordinary ability to hide both his good and bad sentiments—a precious talent indeed, formed by pride and strengthened over time. Meanwhile, little by little, time thinned out his shield, as the battle burgeoned and dragged on. So, the widow's eyes learned to read in his face the terrors and storms of his heart. Occasionally, amidst a trivial, amusing, puerile conversation, Lívia's eyes would darken and her words would die on her lips. The reason for the change would be found in a nearly imperceptible wrinkle she would have discerned in the doctor's face, or in a barely contained gesture, or a poorly disguised glance.

This situation could be hidden from everyone's eyes, but it did not escape those of Luís Batista. Observant and shrewd, yet lacking both passions and scruples, he perceived that the more Félix's love became suspicious and tyrannical, the more terrain he would lose in the widow's heart. With the enchantment thus broken, the hour would arrive for the generous recompense with which he proposed to console the widow over her belated regrets.

To obtain this result, it was necessary to multiply the doctor's suspicions, carve the wound of jealousy deeply into his heart, transform him, in sum, into the instrument of his own ruin. He did not adopt Iago's method, which struck him as risky and childish; rather than insinuating suspicion into Félix's ears, Luís Batista placed it before his eyes.

The difficulty was certainly greater and more elusive, but the suitor possessed on a large scale the qualities necessary to meet it. He must affect a mysterious intimacy with the young woman, discreet, without pomp, all the while infused with infinite caution, so adept she would be caught unawares, but so clearly dissembled it would strike right at Félix's heart.

As for his wife? His wife, my friend, my reader, was a relatively happy young woman. She was beyond resignation, entirely accustomed to her husband's indifference. Providence had bestowed upon her the great virtue of equanimity before life's evils. Clara had sought conjugal happiness, her yearning heart thirsty and hungry for love.

She had not realized her dream. She had asked for a king and was given a log.[29] She accepted the log and asked for nothing more.

Still, Luís Batista had not been a log prior to marriage. He had never felt passion for his fiancée. Instead, his feelings were all his own, a mixture of sensuality and self-satisfaction, a sort of passing fancy, which the first rays of their honeymoon mellowed until they faded completely. Nature reacquired its normal features. Poor little Clara, who had imagined marriage as paradise, saw her dream go up in smoke. She passively accepted the reality she had been given—with no hope, it is true, but also with no regret.

She was lacking—and it was a good thing—the fatal curiosity of the classical amphibian who, disillusioned with the log, asked for a new king, and ended up with a snake, by whom it was swallowed. Virtue saved her from the fall and the shame. She was regretful, perhaps, in the safe haven of her own heart, but she cursed not her destiny. And since she had not the strength to become riled, the household harmony was never disturbed. They could both consider themselves happy creatures.

And thus, since little Clara occupied no place in her husband's soul, he carried out the plan he had designed. The results were slow, but certain. Félix's heart slowly drank the poison his astute rival offered him. Thousands of fortuitous circumstances came to facilitate Luís Batista's scheme. Félix's spirit was perfect terrain for it, his suspicion rarely died in embryo. Once a seed was buried, it sprouted and grew with vigor, overtaking him till the hour of crisis finally loomed, till the hour his rival had been patiently awaiting arrived.

This time Félix made a heroic resolution: to dismantle the beautiful widow's binding allure. Several months had gone by wherein joy and bitterness intermingled. Hundreds of times he convinced himself he had been unjust. But with each new suspicion, all those preceding would reemerge, those she had forgiven. The most recent would then arouse the first, and the poor young man deemed himself hood-winked and ridiculous.

He wrote a long, violent letter wherein he accused the young woman of betrayal and dissimulation. There was bitterness in the letter, as well as hatred and scorn—every-thing meant to wound a heart forever, one that had known love and suffering till then, but could, at length, grow weary and disdainful.

Once it had been sent, he surrendered to his agony, determined not to return to Catumbi. No one saw the tear his desperation wrenched from him, which he has-tened to dry in shame. He then revisited all the goings-on of the previous days, never more convinced of the young woman's treachery, nor of the misery of his own soul. A ray of hope, nevertheless, came and shone through his doubt-filled night. He imagined everything might have been in error and illusion and awaited Lívia's response, that it might elucidate all.

Nothing was elucidated with the young woman's letter, because the letter carrier returned empty-handed. Félix's corrosive jealousy was now accompanied by disdain, a complicated muddle of agony and wounded pride. Lívia appeared to him with all the traits of a vulgar coquette, and a vulgar coquette was not his ideal.

Félix spent the rest of the day in this state. The hours

were long in passing, coldly long as they tend to be for a heart suffering in wait. Finally, evening fell, the sun extinguished everything, the shadows of the night battled the last glimmers of twilight till these were finally overcome.

The melancholy of the hour crept into the doctor's heart and the day's desperation gradually subsided. Félix thought for a long time about his situation, the result of circumstance. He saw the immense space their love had occupied in his life, and the terrible influence it could wield, in the event he were unable to withstand separation. By what means could he escape this outcome, the worst of them all? Félix thought of a trip, as the easiest, most effective means. He was pondering toward this end when he heard a carriage approach.

Shortly thereafter, a servant come in announcing the arrival of someone who insisted on speaking to him: it was a lady.

— A lady! Félix repeated.

It was Lívia. When Félix reached the parlor, she was there at the door, her face covered by a veil, which she lifted immediately. Félix could not contain his surprised gasp.

Lívia was holding a boy's hand, her son. She walked towards the doctor after a few instants of absolute silence and held out her hand.

— You did not expect my visit? she said, entirely composed.

— I must confess, I did not.

— You should have, because I hadn't answered your letter, and it was only fitting I should say something.

— Weren't you concerned about being seen . . . society . . . he said.

— Society's at tea, the widow interjected, trying to smile. It was necessary to come, so I came.

Félix gestured.

— Yes, necessary, Lívia insisted. By now, a letter would have been useless. Between the two of us, letters have lost their virtue, Félix. I no longer know, I no longer have words to reinstate faith in your heart. My boldness perhaps . . .

A glimmer of light fell on the young woman's face. Félix saw two tears quiver in her eyes, hesitate momentarily, then roll down her cheeks, lightly flushed in distress and shame.

— I was perhaps cruel in what I wrote, he said, and I'd like to believe I was also unjust, but I love you. That's my crime in its entirety . . .

Lívia sighed.

— Don't I love you as well? she said. That's no reason for me to be cruel or unfair. But of this I don't accuse you; were that the case I wouldn't be here. I came because I know you're suffering and, in spite of everything, I knew I should come.

Félix led her to the divan and settled into a chair. Luís stood between him and her, somewhat indifferently, and moderately curious at what he was hearing without understanding.

— Weren't you afraid the boy might say something? asked Félix.

— I didn't think of that. I went to visit Raquel, who's not at all well. I went accompanied by him alone. When I thought of coming to Laranjeiras, I was overcome. If I manage to dispel the new doubts afflicting you, I've little concern for the consequences. What do you expect? Thus

is my way. All I see in this world is my love and your joy.
The rest is irrelevant and null.

Lívia said these words in a simple tone, spoken truly
from her soul, which moved the doctor.

— Oh! Then only one thing is needed, said Félix impetuously. Do you swear I had no reason to be suspicious?

Lívia opened her eyes wide, surprised at what she had
heard. She then shook her head in sorrow.

— You, sir, are going to destroy my pride, she said bitterly. I've risked everything to restore your happiness and
peace. You reward my sacrifice with humiliation. Swear to
you! What does one more promise mean between us? If
what I've just done isn't enough, Félix, then let's end our
romance right here. I hope you'll recall at least a page of it
someday, with longing.

Saying these words, the young woman turned away
from him to hide her emotions.

Félix felt a pang of regret, and suddenly felt like falling
at the widow's feet. He murmured a few words, which she
either did not notice or did not hear, until the child caught
the attention of both.

— Let us go, mother?

Lívia stood up and drew the veil over her face.

— Forgive me everything, said Félix. I beg your forgiveness one last time. Don't judge me as others would, if
they only knew the sad story of the past few months. I'm
not bad, I lack trust. Someday hence I'll tell you why. For
now, pardon me again. I've done you wrong, I know so
well. I shouldn't ask anything more of you because you've
so generously given me the greatest consolation my spirit
dared hope for.

— That man? said the widow, after pausing.

— Why do you ask?

— I don't want him in my home, if he calls on me. And I'll avoid occasions where I might meet him.

— He's a man with no respect for you, a libertine, whose wife is an angel . . .

— Doctor Batista?

— The very one.

Lívia offered him her hand. Félix wanted to continue conversing with her, but she observed the lateness of the hour, making her way toward the door. Félix accompanied her to the garden. In bidding her farewell for the last time, the doctor held her hand ardently.

— Forgive me?

— Yes! she said.

And for the first time that night it was her usual tender, loving voice.

Félix watched her enter the carriage, which departed immediately. He went back inside, irritated with himself. He recognized his precipitation and thought himself grossly unjust. If he had carefully considered the young woman's having called on him, he would have realized it was the only way to rid himself of all suspicion. And now that she was gone, he cursed himself for having led her to such an extreme recourse.

The night seemed longer than the day. He was wakeful and had a heavy conscience. He heard the hours clang by one by one, anxious for the next day to arrive so that he could go to Catumbi and redress, through tenderness and respect, the injustice with which he had treated the widow. He closed his eyes as dawn broke through the sky; still, he slept little. When he got up, he was in calmer spirits, and could better evaluate the situation.

"Marriage will restore my trust," he thought; "when the two of us are together, removed from society, from contact with strangers, peace will rule my heart. Only then will we be happy, without bitterness or remorse."

X

The Patient

Raquel's illness was serious. For several days they even feared a fatal outcome. Her elderly parents nearly went out of their minds when the doctor prepared them for the terrible tragedy. The young woman was aware of her own condition, but neither fear of death, nor longing for life on earth caused pain in her heart. She was dying like the flower she was. Her sorrow was for everyone else, who were witnessing her condemnation without recourse.

The attending doctor gave the disease a name either from Greek, or Latin, I'm not sure. Her mother was of the mind there was something beyond the name and the disease. There had been an inexplicable melancholy prior to the illness, a sort of precocious malaise. Raquel had suffered, perhaps, some sort of failed hope—or more clearly put, a hopeless attachment.

To obtain the confession she imagined, Dona Matilde possessed the requisite tact and sweetness. She was a woman and a mother. But, either because Raquel truly did not have anything to confide, or because she wanted to take

71

the secret of her melancholy with her, Raquel divulged nothing.

Two days after Lívia's visit, Félix went to the colonel's house. The colonel was in the parlor, sunk into a chair, his eyes still and his expression worn with the vigil and pain. He tried to get up when Félix appeared at the door, but Félix rushed to him and prevented him from doing so.

— I learned yesterday of your daughter's grave state, said Félix, sitting down next to the old man. I've heard she's doing poorly . . .

— Poorly, the colonel repeated, definitively, poorly. The doctor's dashed the slight hope we had. You cannot know what it's like to lose half of one's soul.

Félix said a few banalities by way consolation, and even mentioned hopes. Yet, even if hope always penetrates the hearts of the wretched, by then the good old man believed in nothing more than death.

For some time they were quiet, until the colonel finally broke the silence.

— You are a dear friend to Raquel, he said. Twice, she's asked about you.

— How long has she been ill?

— She took to her bed fifteen days ago, but she'd been suffering prior to that. At first, I paid little mind. Her malady worsened rapidly, though, and its only gotten more serious.

They were interrupted by the doctor attending Raquel. The man in question had a been at school with Félix. Upon seeing Félix, he imagined his former colleague had been called in. Félix rushed to explain his visit.

— Nonetheless, Doctor Félix, I'll take advantage of

your insights, and perhaps we could compare our impressions, if you're in agreement.

The colonel went to see if Raquel was awake. He returned shortly and accompanied the two doctors to her room.

Félix was the first to cross the threshold. He paused momentarily, moved by the spectacle before him.

Dona Matilde was sitting at the head of the bed, pallid and weary, her eyes swollen, perhaps from crying. At the foot of the bed there sat a young woman, Raquel's childhood friend and, on this occasion, her devoted nurse. Both of them contemplated the patient in silence and sorrow.

Raquel was as white as the bed linen where she rested her lovely head. Her lips were parted and her breath was short and troubled. The slight commotion of the doctors entering her room startled her. Raquel opened her eyes, which were burning with fever.

When Félix approached the bed and took the young woman's wrist, she looked at him, gesturing in fear. Then she looked around, as if she were in doubt as to her whereabouts. Dona Matilde leaned towards her daughter.

— It's Doctor Félix.

Raquel looked at Félix again, with the faint, sad smile of the ailing.

— Thank you! she murmured.

— How are you feeling? asked Félix.

— Better, she said in a voice so frail it was at most a sigh.

— Truly better?

Raquel gestured indifferently, without answering.

— Now, now, don't give up, said Félix, and above all, don't make your parents sad, they love you so much.

Félix examined the patient, asking her some questions, to which she responded weakly. When he finished questioning her, the young woman murmured.

— I'm dying, right?

— No, said Félix, you won't die, you cannot die. You have a long life ahead of you, but you must have the will to live.

Raquel gestured in disbelief at the doctor's kind words, her eyes seeking her mother. Dona Matilde's penetrated Félix, as if she wanted to read in his face her daughter's sentence. The patient seemed to divine her mother's thoughts, then she spoke with effort.

— And, why don't you offer my mother your consolation?

The parley did not last long. Félix began by offering the opinion that there should be some changes in the treatment thus far. He declared he did not believe all hope was lost. His colleague agreed readily to the recommended modifications, all the more so, he added, since there was no hope.

In his opinion, Raquel was irremediably lost. It was not a flimsy, nor unfounded opinion. He could prove it with thorough, irrefutable arguments. He made his case effectively for twenty minutes, with the correct assessment of the facts, sure scientific data, and a dialectic so sound it was impossible to raise the slightest objection.

Fifteen days later, Raquel was recovering.

As far as for her parents, they thought of Félix as their daughter's savior. He had restored their faith and had done so with his good advice and unfailing kindness.

Félix's colleague, for whom the young woman's revival meant the destruction of all the medical notions he had learned, was profoundly surprised with the result. In any case, it was impossible to deny it. He limited himself to applauding it and, when the young woman began convalescing, he advised the parents to send her away from the city, for fresh air.

The advice could not have been more opportune. Lívia had relocated to Laranjeiras. The idea for the move was Viana's, who one day proposed it to his sister, by whom it was approved. The house was up the road from Félix's, on the opposite side.

It was elegantly constructed, set in the middle of a fine estate,[30] neither extensive nor overly groomed. Viana, meanwhile, organized a series of improvements, which he promised to carry out forthwith. His satisfaction seemed boundless. Aside from preferring that neighborhood to where they had previously lived, there was the circumstance of finding themselves so near to Félix's house— which was already half their joy, as he said.

Lívia approved the move for the same reasons. The foregoing days had been deliciously peaceful. Her future projects were endless. She envisaged a life disencumbered of all social drudgery, a life for themselves, replete with the exaltation of poetry and love. At times she feared her dreams were only that, dreams. Even so, she would not have exchanged them for anything in the world.

So there they were, in the early days of October. The marriage had been set for mid-January, set—lest there be no misunderstanding—strictly between the two of them, since Félix had managed to extract the promise from the widow that the news would only be shared days prior to the event.

— But why the secrecy? Lívia asked upon agreeing to his request.

— Mere whim.

The real reason was the vacillation in his soul, but the one he gave perfectly satisfied the young woman.

— If I had your heart, she said, I'd mistrust your request; but, alas, I do trust you.

They were by themselves on the estate. Viana, in keeping with his idea to leave the two lovers undisturbed, had remained at a distance, overseeing his planned improvements. They thus walked alone, silently, distractedly—rather, entirely absorbed in each other. Suddenly, the widow looked up, as if continuing her previous conjecture.

— Still, on occasion this trust may be shaken, not because I doubt you, but because I doubt destiny. I've already told you I'm superstitious—a female, childish flaw. Sometimes, when I think about the future, I shiver . . . beset with doubt, I ask myself how this will all end. Perhaps it's the faintness of my heart, my ambitions, far exceeding the obtainable.

— Don't you think I've mended my ways? said Félix, smiling. How many days has it been since . . .

— Hush! Lívia interrupted him, touching his lips with her fingers. I fear your carrying on so.

And after a minute of silence . . .

— It's not your heart that makes me tremble, for you have a fine heart. Nor is it your soul, although capricious, visionary, and inconstant. I fear the future, in light of the past.

— The past? asked Félix, stopping abruptly.

Lívia sighed.

— And what was amiss in your past? the doctor continued, staring at her with accusatory eyes.

— Everything.

There was an old straw-plaited settee nearby. Lívia walked slowly toward him and sat down. Félix contemplated her for some time from where he had remained. He was no longer smiling, a shadow of doubt cast over his eyes. Finally, he took a few steps and stopped before her.

XI

The Past

— Would it be indiscreet of me to inquire about this past? asked Félix after several moments.

— Oh! Rest assured! There's nothing weighing on my conscience, but on my heart . . .

— Did you love someone?

— I loved my husband.

Lívia's response was followed by a long silence. The memory of the past to which she had so mysteriously alluded seemingly troubled her soul. Her breast was pounding and her hands, which the doctor touched lovingly, were icy and trembling.

— And you don't believe I've a greater understanding of you than the others? the doctor finally inquired.

— Perhaps not.

Félix gestured in annoyance. The young woman gathered her dress, allowing space for the doctor to sit beside her on the sofa, where he settled.

— Perhaps you don't understand me any better than the others, continued Lívia, and by that I don't mean to say you're as common or even more so than they are. You aren't. Still, there are some things a man is at pains to comprehend, I believe.

— Even when in love? Asked Félix.

Lívia did not respond.

— But what past was this? Félix continued. I may not understand you, as you claim, but I would know how to speak a few words of consolation, how to dispel the remaining sorrow of this secret, which is not regret, most certainly.

— I loved my husband, Lívia began, and my entire secret is bound up in those few words. I experienced the passion of youth, when love arrives taking unknowing hearts by surprise. Could this love be stronger? Some say first loves are born of the mere need to love. Possibly. Now that I love you, I sense it might be so. In any case, that affection took hold of me entirely. I relished a life I thought immortal.

— And he?

— I believe he loved me, but we didn't share the same notion of love, such was my painful, belated disenchantment. For me love was divine ecstasy, a sort of dream taking on a life of its own, an absolute transformation from soul to soul; whilst for him, love was a moderate feeling—a prudent, conjugal pretense, without fervor, nor wings, nor illusions . . . Perhaps we both erred, who knows?

— I see you were incompatible, Félix interrupted. But why hold everyone to your manner of seeing and feeling, which stems more from the imagination than reality?

Lívia shrugged her shoulders.

— I'm explaining, revealing my soul, she continued.

I was troubled and sad, I didn't hide it from him. And he laughed, an apathetic, cold man. It's true he was honest and kind-hearted, but we spoke in different languages and couldn't understand each other. Still, I believed in the persuasion of love. I endeavored to draw him into my feelings, a mistaken effort that brought me only suffering and fatigue. I disheartened him with what he called poetic silliness. His weariness was soon exasperation, and then it went from exasperation to boredom. The day boredom set in, I realized the evil was done. I tried to make amends, but I'd transformed our married life into a desert. If my soul cried out against this destiny, my conscience accused me of my own mistake, the mistake of having disturbed domestic peace in exchange for a chimeric dream. I don't make myself out to be better than I am, surely you can see that. Yet, mightn't my guilt be, in part, the fault of nature for making me so puerile? Such is my fear now, continued Lívia after a few seconds of silence, at times I think I didn't come into this world to be happy, nor to make anyone else happy. I was born with this flaw, it seems. Would you be able to quell this apprehension, amend my flaw?

The widow concluded, holding out her hand to the doctor, who clasped it between his. A sympathetic or tender smile, perhaps a combination of the two, formed on Félix's lips. Neither one of them spoke. They seemed to be talking to themselves. Finally, the widow repeated her question.

— Perhaps I can dispel your apprehension, responded Félix. But I fear it won't be easy. You still have the heart of a child, and probably will till you die, I think.

Félix was quiet, contemplating the widow's countenance

at length. She was looking down, absorbed and pensive.
Little by little the doctor's face became equally grave. For a
long while they allowed themselves to follow the current of
their somber thoughts. Félix was the first to awake from
this torpor.

— You've been shipwrecked with land in sight, he said,
and you've emerged with nothing worse than a dampened
dress. Do you know what it is to be shipwrecked on the
high sea, alone, losing everything, your very life? That's
how it was for me.

— Yes? said Lívia, her voice a blend of joy and curiosity.

Félix could not contain his smile. "How selfish are the
unhappy . . ." he thought.

He continued:

— Yes, I lost a lot more. To embrace a corpse, what is
that to one who's embraced a snake? You merely lost a few
years of misunderstood love. You didn't lose a precious
good, stolen from me by time: trust. You can still find the
happiness you once yearned for. It's enough for you to
love someone. While I, my dear Lívia, lack the principle
element of inner peace, for I don't trust in the sincerity
of others.

Here he stopped, as if he were expecting some response
from the widow. She, though, was watching him peacefully, even smilingly. Félix continued imparting the secrets
of his past, accounts of thwarted affections and deceit told
with sincere expansiveness, as if he were talking to himself. At times, his emotion caused his voice to falter and,
especially in these moments, one could read the rapture in
the widow's eyes as she listened to him speaking his heart.

— No one was ever so generous in squandering his

affection as I was, the doctor continued, no one knew better than I how to be both friend and lover. I was as trusting as you are, hypocrisy, betrayal, and egoism were never more to me than regrettable aberrations. My spirit created a world of its own, a platonic society, where fraternity was the universal language, and love, the law of the land. I allowed myself to go on so, down the river of years, expending the entire lifeblood of my youth, with no calculation nor regret, until I was struck by fatal disenchantment.

He was quiet. He sensed movement nearby; it was Viana who was strolling the grounds, absorbed in his horticultural plans. Would he have heard Félix's voice? It seems so, because he gradually moved away from them. The two were left alone again. The doctor continued.

— My illusions did not drop like dry leaves, plucked and carried off by a feeble breeze, they were torn from me in the vigor of their bloom. They left me with no sweet memories, the breath of life for ailing souls. My spirits were arid and dry, engulfed in cruel misanthropy. At first, irritated and violent, then melancholy and resignation set in. My soul was gradually made callous, and my heart literally died.

Félix continued his recitation in this same plaintive, sad tone. It was long and true. Had the widow been listening with more than her heart, she might have perceived something beyond resentment and bitterness. Félix was not intrinsically bad. He was, however, disdainfully or hypocritically skeptical, depending on the circumstances. Not only would she have perceived this, she would also have realized nature had somehow played a hand in the

doctor's moral transformation. His lack of trust in sentiments and people was not solely due to the deceptions that
had come his way, it also had its roots in the inertia of his
spirit and the feebleness of his heart. His energy was an
act of will, not an innate characteristic; he was above all
weak and capricious.

Lívia perceived none of this. She listened to him with
the devout faith of a loving heart. Realizing his current
dejection was caused by his past misfortunes, she trusted
herself with the renewal of that soul, so prematurely aged.
Such were her consolations when the doctor ended his
long confidences. He thanked her emotionally, but not
without asking her if she had enough strength to under-
take the pious mission.

— I do, Lívia said confidently.

— It's certain you'll revive me, the doctor continued,
if the future still holds for me some days of pure joy, I'll
owe them to you alone, my dear Lívia, you alone will have
achieved the miracle. But . . .

— But? the young woman repeated impatiently.

— The work is incomplete, Félix continued, only half-
way finished. You've caused a solitary, but beautiful flower
to bloom among the ruins. It's unique in the arid land of
my heart. But it's not enough, now it needs a ray of light to
rouse it and keep it thriving. This would be the trust established not over an hour's time, rather, every single day—a
trust that never dies and will restore our past serenity.
Without it, my love will be but vast, useless martyrdom.

As he said this, he held her to his chest, nearly allowing
their languid faces to touch lightly, not out of voluptuous-
ness, but rather, out of tenderness. This moment of mutual

contemplation was brief, yet in practice, was worth many hours. If life were forever composed of such moments, Félix's heart would most probably have obtained the peace he so coveted. The young woman finally relinquished herself, as if the weight of those exuberant emotions had left her weakened, and words flowed from their lips.

They spoke then in prose, of their future projects, the wedding arrangements, the trip they were to take immediately following. They were about to rise when, from a distance, Lívia's brother appeared. Viana walked briskly and cheerfully to meet the two lovers. Félix set his facial expression according to the requirements of the circumstances. As he approached, Viana told his sister that Colonel Morais was in the parlor with his daughter.

Lívia excused herself to the doctor and headed toward the house. Félix offered Viana his arm.

— We were discussing your improvements, he said, prosaically calculating future expenses.

Viana smiled disguisedly, clinging to the subject at hand. He spoke animatedly of his plans, which were vast and original, concluding with a simple confession, accompanied by a questioning regard.

— I'm afraid, he said, that Lívia will marry sooner or later.

Félix limited himself to smiling indifferently as they entered the parlor.

XII

A Black Spot

Lívia and Raquel were seated on the sofa. Settled in an armchair, the colonel was consulting his watch. He was not in fact consulting it, rather, holding it before his eyes. In matter of fact, though, his eyes were set on his daughter as she answered the widow's questions.

— Here's the patient, said Lívia, upon seeing the doctor and her brother appear in the doorway.

Raquel turned her head, and could not contain an exclamation of surprise and joy.

Félix stepped forward to take her hand.

— So, she's cured, is she not? he said, looking alternately at the two young ladies.

— It was you who saved her, sir, said the colonel, drawing near the group.

— Not at all, I only helped nature, nothing more.

— We're going to see to it she makes a full recovery, and regains her lively ways, said Lívia, bestowing a kiss on the patient.

Raquel listened to this exchange with a sad smile,

seemingly sadder for emanating from those colorless lips.
She was extremely wan and thin. Her eyes, now that the
feverish blaze had been extinguished, appeared sunken and
dead. Nonetheless, she had not lost her natural refine-
ment. What is more, the very morbidity of her appearance
showed her off to advantage.

Perhaps those circumstances affected the doctor's newly
formed impression. For the first time, Raquel appeared to
him as a woman.

The colonel breathed contentment throughout his
pores. The happiness he had lost during his daughter's
illness had now returned, more boisterous and expansive
than ever. He was a jovial, talkative old gent, fond of rep-
artee and yarns, more amusing than coarse, endowed with
that amiable earnestness that leads to familiarity with no
loss of respect. Every once in a while, he would look at his
daughter, eyes filled with paternal love, seeming to forget
the rest of the world, because the entire world, at least
part of it—because the other part had stayed home—was
composed of that slender, weakened being.

— And promise me you'll revive her for me, he said
to the widow, not so she's rosy, which she never was, but
healthy looking, lively like she used to be, and happy, and,
who knows, even mischievous?

— And why not? There's the fine air, tender care, and,
better still than fresh air and gentle care, nature will surely
work its cure and, I believe, so will her own efforts . . . Isn't
that so? said Lívia, patting Raquel on her cheek.

Raquel answered her with a kiss, and a smile, no longer sad like the first one. Dusk had fallen completely. The
colonel made some final recommendations to his daughter, thanked the widow and the doctor, climbed into his

carriage, and returned to Catumbi. Lívia went to show her friend to her room. Félix said his farewells to the two ladies and made his way toward the door.

— You'll return? asked Lívia.

— Perhaps not, madam, answered Félix, who fully intended to be back to take tea.

Raquel's presence had somehow altered the relations between the two lovers. Their solitary meetings, when they forgot both the world and themselves, could no longer be so frequent. More than ever, Félix tried to conceal his love from others' observation so that, in spite of spending a great deal of time with them both, Raquel suspected nothing between them. Raquel might have guessed at something had she noticed the widow spoke almost exclusively of the doctor when the two ladies conversed. Nevertheless, since Raquel too spoke of no one else, to her it seemed the widow was merely following her lead.

Around this time Meneses began to frequent the home of Viana, with whom he had established relations several months prior. Félix spoke of Meneses sincerely and deservedly in the highest terms. The parasite seconded the doctor's good opinion of Meneses with the enthusiasm emanating from the aroma of delicious dinners. Meneses also met the widow's expectations and before long became a regular caller.

Meneses was cured of his ill-fated passion. Cured and irritated, he would say, when Félix inquired as to the situation.

— These loves are like school-boys' lessons, concluded Meneses, smiling. You've already concluded primary school, why don't you advance your studies?

To this somewhat overworked metaphor, Félix

responded with a smile, at once a confession and a negation. Meneses, who had no ulterior motives, did not
bother to investigate which of the expressions suited his
friend's smile. Their relations seemed to grow closer. Were
he a bit more expansive and trustful, the doctor would
have mentioned his loves and his forthcoming happiness.
He did not, though, nor did Meneses wonder. He did
harbor suspicion one night when he caught the widow's
loving gaze, penetrating the doctor, but the indifference
with which the latter stood up to converse jokingly with
Raquel dissuaded him entirely.

Days went by, long for the two lovers, short for Meneses
and Raquel, who found within that house the most
delightful company in the world.

Here the novel might end naturally and traditionally,
marrying the two pairs of hearts and dispatching them off
to enjoy the honeymoon in some faraway place unknown
to man. But for that, impatient reader, it would have been
necessary for the colonel's daughter and Doctor Meneses to
be in love with each other, which they were not, nor were
they inclined to such sentiments. One reason Meneses's
eyes were drawn away from that lovely girl was that they
were enamored of the widow. By way of admiration or
love? Initially, admiration, and later, love—a circumstance
for which neither he, nor the author, is to be blamed.
What to do? She was beautiful and young, he was youth-
ful and enamored. Furthermore, whether naïve or blind,
he did not intuit the previously existing relation between
the widow and the doctor, still under the veils with which
they hid it from him.

Contrary to Félix, whose spirit only begot misgivings
and doubt, above all, Meneses was given to rose-colored

fantasies. These fit together like playthings in his imagination. Meneses readily glimpsed a world of hope. The widow's affability in her relations with him seemed auspicious. The most innocent of smiles served him as the foundation for a castle in the sky. Any slight expression, mere salon politesse, seemed to him replete with a thousand future promises. There was neither future nor hope, only his candor, which was but a rosebud, still partially closed to life's corruption.

Such was the contrast between the characters of the two men, whom the widow's star—I cannot say whether it was good or bad—had united on their knees before her. One of the men, in adoring an artificial countenance, might sink further into degradation, his eyes still fixed on chimeric joy; the other, burning for the most angelic of human creatures, would break with his own two hands the ladder that could lead him to heaven.

At length, Félix realized the inner workings of his friend's heart. His first impression was ire, not for precipitated doubt respecting the young woman, for it was this very reason another dared love her. And wasn't such a situation dangerous? A simple question sufficed for his spirit to take flight. His immediate inference was that the young woman did not find Meneses's lovemaking unpleasant. First vanity, then habit, and finally the predilection of the heart would lead them one to the other. Perhaps they already had.

On one occasion, in talking about Lívia, Meneses's expression went abruptly from humorous to grave. Félix was more skilled than he, it was not difficult to probe the depths of Meneses's heart. His friend told him everything, with his characteristic fervor, and the ingenuousness of a man still not conversant with the ways of the world. The doctor listened to him anxiously, but apparently unmoved.

— As for prospects?

— Few or many, I'm not certain which. At times it seems to me everything is easy and decisive, at others, I'm discouraged and don't even believe in myself. She's pleasant to me, but so she is to you and to everyone else. Has she already guessed? I'd like to believe she has, and since she's not vexed, it's a good omen, or so I believe. The worst of all is, I've not the courage to tell her what I feel.

Just one word would have been enough for the doctor to remove the nascent rival from his path. Félix rejected the idea, part cunning, part pride—misplaced pride, but true to his nature. The cunning was worse, a sort of strata-gem—an experiment, he would say—to place before each other two souls that seemed to him, in a word, kindred... to tempt them both, and then appraise Lívia's constancy and sincerity.

And thus, he was the craftsman of his own misfortune. He gathered in his hands the elements of the fire in which he was to burn, if not in reality, at least in fantasy, because any evil that did not yet exist, he himself would produce from nothing, in order to render it vital and forceful.

Meneses further explained the workings of his soul. It was not violent love he felt, rather serene and tender affec-tion, a peaceful, yet irresistible fascination. The doctor, through a remaining sense of decorum, did not openly encourage his friend's longings. Nonetheless, his words were so joyful, his laughter so genuine, that Meneses's hopeful spirit flourished once again if, indeed, it had ever languished.

XIII
Crisis

Lívia did not immediately perceive Meneses's love, but it was impossible that she not suspect, sooner or later. After a period of pursuit, she did not dissemble when he confided in her in Laranjeiras. She showed neither surprise nor irritation. Moreover, apart from not rousing anger, there was between the two of them—as Félix had commented one day—a certain conformity of sentiment and thought, which in one way or another linked them.

The answer she gave Meneses was firmly cold and decisive, not disdainful, nor severe. Still, when she perceived herself to be the motive of such sorrow, she cast aside all conventional and requisite formalities. She tried to smooth the young man's feathers. She dashed his hopes, present and future; she would never be able to love him. Their friendship however, which she held in esteem, might assuage his disillusion. That was all. She should not feign a love she did not feel, nor hint at joy she was unable to give him.

— That you cannot give me! repeated Meneses, still

clinging to fleeting hopes, and if I were to await the
day the happiness you now deny me is fulfilled? Nothing
depends on us alone. The very movements of the heart seem
to be born of a thousand chance circumstances, if they aren't
somehow mysteriously orchestrated, and thus . . . who
knows? Maybe someday—I dare to believe it—one day
you'll feel the sympathy I inspire in you has transformed,
and . . .

— That's enough! Lívia cut him off imperiously.

Meneses ceased, and she carried on.

— Love is not what you, sir, say it is. It's not born of
chance circumstance, nor of lengthy intimacy, rather it's
harmony between two natures, who recognize and com-
plement each other. No matter how similar our spirit may
be, I do not feel God intended for us to be united in love.

Meneses was not disposed to such theoretical mean-
derings. It is even doubtful whether or not he paid much
attention to the widow's last words. He saw the chimerical
castle he had so laboriously constructed go up in smoke,
and by then, that was his sole impression.

Some time went by of absolute, restrained silence. They
were leaning out the window overlooking the garden.
Meneses did not dare lift his eyes to her. It was not only
his embarrassment, prosaic, given the situation he found
himself in. It was also fear of contemplating, yet again, the
goodness he had lost. Lívia was sympathetic to the young
man's spirits—perhaps even regretful he was not the young
man her heart had chosen. Who knows? And finally, there
came the most she could give him, and it was a lot.

— We'll remain friends, she said. Our friendship will
make you forget your love, it's gentler and perhaps less

likely to perish. I admit my egotism, in asking you something that will benefit me alone. Friends—you'll have no
difficulty finding them; but the same is not true for me,
and certainly not friends such as yourself.

Meneses touched her hand lightly as she held it out
to him with her last words. The request she made of him
was more affectionate than judicious. A disillusioned heart
knows not immediate compensation, nor effective consolation. The widow's kindness moved him nonetheless. He
was on the verge of thanking her when Raquel entered
the room.

Raquel stopped short. They were both flustered. The
widow was the first to break the silence, addressing the colonel's daughter. What was the significance of that benevolent, yet cunning smile emerging from her lips? Meneses,
who was looking outside, did not see it, but the widow
did, and shuddered.

Meneses did not return for a week. He would have
prolonged his absence if love, that breeding ground of
illusions, had not filled his heart with renewed hope. Lívia
treated him with her usual cordiality, perhaps even more
so. Since Félix's trust had not wavered, Lívia practiced a
sort of honest dissimulation, out of plain goodness and gratitude. This manner of construing the situation was innate to
her character; she managed with little regard for social con-
vention. Ingenuous, is how I would describe her, if I were to
explain the true sentiments of the widow, who believed her
kind comportment was a sort of spiritual mission.

I wish upon the missionaries of this breed, if they exist,
more discernment or a luckier star. Neither our heroine's
discernment nor her luck was stronger than her heart.

The sentiments driving her were good, only her proce-
dure was wrong. She did not take this into consideration.
She studied the doctor's face, which was more confident
and cheerful than ever, and this alone filled her eyes. Had
her eyes been less enamored, they would have perceived
Félix's calm to be so exaggerated and out of character, it
could not possibly be sincere.

To these errors and illusions, sufficient components for
the impending drama, were joined Raquel's illusion. She
sincerely applauded the sentiments she attributed to the
widow in relation to Meneses. Her smile upon catching
them unawares meant nothing less. On one occasion, her
impression led her to press the widow. And the urgency
of Lívia's response only confirmed Raquel's suspicions. In
that moment, Lívia wanted to divulge everything, the true
object of her love, and her imminent wedding but, even
though they were close in age, Lívia considered Raquel still
a child and refrained.

Raquel maintained her suspicions.

Let us now pardon the poor young woman's lack of
experience—a mere child, as the widow would have said—
and her levity as she insinuated her suspicions to the doctor. Requesting a word with him, she did it by way of a
delicate, elegant allusion. His shock was profound. This
time the proof seemed decisive.

Raquel noticed the doctor's reaction. The innocent,
playful smile starting to form on her lips was suddenly
gone. Félix looked at her, oblivious to the change that had
come over her. He finally perceived it, yet remained in the
dark. He attempted his usual playful manner with her and
managed to make her smile.

The following days were a sad trial for the widow. We already know that Félix's jealousy was harsh at times. Never before had it been so terrible. Lengthy letters were exchanged—hers, bitter, his coldly cruel and disparaging. Félix was not forthwith in revealing the cause of this renewed crisis. Lívia guessed, and she told him everything faithfully, without omitting her good intentions to spare Meneses's heart. Hardly the ways of a woman. Félix saw it all as a web of absurdities.

What he then said was but a transcription of the letters he had sent her. Rudeness, irony, incoherency, all contained in the words he chose to annihilate the poor woman.

Lívia did not protest. She tried to interrupt him only once. By the time he finished, she found nothing left deserving of a response. They were in the parlor. She looked around at all the doors, frightened, then collapsed into a chair, covering her face with her hands.

Félix took a step towards her. It was a fine motion, but his regret was instantaneous.

— Farewell! he said.

The young woman uncovered her face.

— Félix! she exclaimed.

The doctor stopped several seconds. Lívia stood up and approached him rashly. She managed to take one of his hands; tearful and defeated, she was on the verge of making one last plea. But he pulled his hand away violently, looked at her, and after a long silence, repeated . . .

— Farewell!

XIV

A Chapter of Happenstance

Félix arrived home irascible and desperate. He entered the room impetuously. As if he somehow had to avenge the purported wrongdoing, he reached for the first vase he came across and threw it on the floor. The vase shattered.

— What's going on? said a strange voice.

Félix was caught by surprise. He looked at the window, from where he had heard the voice, and met with the sight of Moreirinha, seated comfortably, with an open book of etchings on his knees.

— It's me, said the visitor, getting up and going to shake Félix's hand. Are you surprised to find me here? I took the liberty of waiting for you, despite your servant's recommendation.

Félix was unable to contain his displeasure at this visit. Moreirinha read this clearly in his eyes and continued.

— Perhaps my presence is unwelcome, especially since it seems to me you've something bothering you, but I had no choice . . .

Félix shrugged his shoulders.

— And your displeasure will be even greater, Moreirinha
continued, when you understand my request for shelter is
not for just one hour, but till tomorrow.

In saying this, he extended his hand. Félix extended
his and told him coldly he could stay as long as he liked.

For a suffering heart, there is nothing more bothersome
than indifferent, frivolous conversation. The circumstances
only further embittered Félix's spirits. Solitude may have
been a salutary balm, if there were such a thing for him.
Chance, however, had confronted him with a witness
before whom he had to feign the equanimity he did not
command.

His guest understood the situation, and told him
frankly he meant not to disturb him. He had come seeking asylum, not as a visitor, knowing he had no right to his
host's consideration. Félix responded as well as he could to
this courtesy which, by the way, only increased his obligation. With no means of escape, he tried at least to correspond. Moreover, Moreirinha was not as importune as he
might have been, because he talked unceasingly, evading
the foible of the typical nuisance, who inquiringly inter-
rupts discourse at every turn . . . by way of mouth and
gesture.

Before long, the guest divulged what had brought him
there. It was Cecília. In spite of the circumstances in which
Félix found himself, he could not contain his interest.

— Cecília? he asked.

— It's true. It's my ruinous angel. Do you remember
how I praised her? I was sincere, it was all true at the time.
Till then, I'd never come across such sweetness. I'm not

maudlin you know, but I'm inclined to such episodes. I
don't know what they did to the poor girl, she's entirely
changed, the devil incarnate. Those chains that held us to
each other—so light I used to call them chains of roses—
well, they're now chains of heavy iron. I want to escape her,
but I can't. I've tried everything, all in vain. I hide myself
away at home, at friends' houses, at hotels. No matter
where I go, she's sure to find me, and then God knows
what I go through. Today it dawned on me I could come
here, spend the rest of the afternoon and evening with you.
I'm certain she won't catch up with me.

Félix listened attentively to Moreirinha's explanation,
not without drawing some comparison between his own
state and that of his guest. Moreirinha then narrated several episodes illustrating what he called his servitude.

— And you don't know of any way to escape her for
once and for all?

— None. Even if I could leave Rio de Janeiro, I'm certain she'd find me on board a ship or at the door of the
carriage I'd take to get there.

Such a significant change in Cecília's character did not
fail to capture Félix's attention. He easily perceived it to be
the work of the lover himself. The turtledove had become
a hawk, for the simple reason that Moreirinha had allowed
it to realize its own strength.

From one defeat to the next, Moreirinha had arrived at
his current miserable state. He was not a forceful man, nor
one to engage in philosophical musings. He was very much
a man to flee and postpone—his character was made up
of inertia and fear, marvelously disposed to useless despair
and shameful capitulation.

— But why don't you leave the Capital[31] for a while? said Félix after a few minutes. There must be some way to escape . . .

Moreirinha reflected for a moment.

— There are two reasons, he said. The first is, regardless of everything, I'm still fond of her and, if I could escape her for thirty days, on the thirty-first, I'd seek her out . . .

— And the second reason, interrupted Félix who seemed bothered by this ingenuous confession.

— The second reason? responded Moreirinha with some hesitation, is that . . . I can't.

Félix glanced down at the young man's attire and saw there a commentary on the words he had just heard. There was still elegance, but now poor and frayed. Moreirinha's shoes showed signs of long wear, his finely tailored coat was made of visibly inferior fabric. He was wearing light brown gloves, but it did not escape Félix's curious gaze that the fingertips were already smeared with black slime, the vestige of persistent use.

There was no need for great acumen to realize it was entirely due to Cecília's doing. Nor would it be too far off the mark were someone to bet Moreirinha was forever-more condemned to that woman's caprice. One thing was certain, the young man was unable to satisfy all her vanity and needs. She had taken it upon herself to access sources beyond her planned disbursement, through a judiciously calculated system of taxation.

Félix understood this at a glance and attempted to lift Moreirinha's spirits with happier thoughts, more for himself than for his guest.

It was done with little difficulty. Moreirinha's spirit had

a natural aversion to grave ruminations. He took up the opportunity the doctor provided and began discussing the day's events. As for the thousands of episodes in the life of a certain set, there was no one better informed than Cecília's lover. The new loves of this girl, the quarrels of another, the amusing remarks of yet another, the affair of still one more, he knew it all first hand. Better not ask him about new literary works nor political crises, but the furniture that Tom had bestowed upon a certain lady, and the dubious supper at which Dick had even drunk champagne out of a lady's shoe, this was his terrain, ever since Cecília's passion had completely detached him from society.

This was neither amusing nor interesting, but it filled the time and, since he was obliged to suffer his guest, it was better to do so in this manner.

It was impossible, however, for Félix's spirits not to idle on his own plight. Every once in a while, the doctor would forget the narrator, and his mind would flutter about the widow. In precisely such a moment, a letter from her arrived. Félix opened it eagerly and read it twice through. It was long, recounting the history of those previous months, and concluding with an appeal to the doctor's reason. One can imagine the young woman wrote with tears in her eyes, but no longer in the entreating tone she had used when attempting reconciliation in similar situations.

Time had worked some effect on Félix's soul, and the letter served to finalize that development. He was not yet certain of the widow's innocence, but was already very certain of the brutality of his outburst, and this recognition caused him further pain, almost as deep as what he had suffered initially.

His first impulse was to go to Lívia. He resisted, though, preferring to write her a letter. Three times he began without managing to finish. He vacillated between affection and severity. In one case he recalled her possible betrayal, in the other, her probable innocence. He feared being unfair or ridiculous. Like all indecisive characters, he found no other recourse but useless desperation.

Night fell. Moreirinha was more jovial than ever, repaying the doctor's hospitality with his customary jokes. He was not expecting Cecília, but guessed it was she when he heard a carriage stop at the door.

— I'm lost! he said with a long sigh.

It was her.

Weary of waiting for someone to bring her his response, Cecília stepped down from the carriage and entered the house. Upon reaching the doorway, she glanced around the room, where she did not at first see her lover. Moreirinha had placed himself within the frame of one of the windows. Félix looked severely at Cecília, demonstrating his discomfort at the liberty she had taken. Oh, but where are the flowers of yesteryear?[32] The sweet young lady of former times had become a wanton, fallen woman. She headed boldly towards the doctor, offering him her hand.

— How are you, *mon vieux?*[33] she said, laughing mockingly.

At this point, she discovered the presence of her lover, who seemed otherwise occupied, counting the stars. She went to him, preparing her vehemently pleading words, at which point Félix decided it would be prudent to intervene, to stave off possible scandal. He reconciled them to the best of his ability and dryly dismissed them.

Lívia was looking out the window, disconsolate and sad, while Raquel, no less sorrowful than Lívia, played a piece on the piano fitting to the two young women's state of mind. The doctor's answer had not arrived. Lívia felt her hopes of the past several months fading away and, along with them, the future that had seemed so within her reach. These were her melancholy thoughts when she saw a carriage stopping in front of Félix's door. She saw a woman step down and enter the house, then leave it, accompanied by a man, with whom she departed.

The blow was terrible, deeper than ever. Surely the widow did not fear a triumphant rival. Nonetheless, she saw and felt the disregard of the man over whom she had shed so many tears that day. If the doctor were to have appeared right then, she would have realized her mistake, and the joy at feeling admired would have strengthened her resolve to disregard the pain of having been offended. Félix did not come. Lívia could hardly withstand the humiliation. One tear—her last—was the only expression of her immense despair.

XV

Enfant Terrible

The following day, first thing, Viana went to the doctor's house. He was not planning to lunch with him. He intended to invite him to dinner.

— It's my birthday today, said the parasite, and I'd like to gather a very few friends around my table. You, sir, are among the first, don't let me down.

— I won't, Félix answered.

Viana went on to express several ideas regarding how one should brave a birthday dinner. It should include intimate friends exclusively, since it was offered from the heart, and informal merrymaking, wherein any talk less than that of friendship would be foreign, even adverse. Taste was not enough in choosing such friends. One needed skill and wisdom to differentiate between attachments of affection and those based on habit. He had forgotten the most important thing, he had forgotten to say that, from his point of view, a birthday dinner was also an investment.

Félix accepted the invitation eagerly. He had been waiting for a pretext to return to Lívia's house. He was still tormented with jealousy, but his irritation had subsided. It had been replaced by the desire to reestablish their former harmony, not through his own doing, but through a complete explanation from his loved one.

With these sentiments, he left his house. Lívia was looking out her window when she saw him arriving. She met him on the landing of the stairway leading down to the garden. She pressed his hand with a sorrowful smile.

— I'm the one who should forgive you, she said, but it would wound your pride.

— My pride? Forgive me? Félix repeated.

— Yes, she said, with an affirmative nod.

Félix read in her face such sincere composure; he was on the verge of reconciliation. He hesitated for a moment when, in glancing into the parlor, he saw Raquel approaching the stairway. He then recalled what she had confided to him in tacit secrecy and answered Lívia bitterly.

— Let us be serious.

Lívia paled. She wanted to respond, but could not. Raquel was with them.

A short while later, the colonel and Dona Matilde arrived. Meneses followed soon after. A few others made up the party. The presence of strangers constrained the widow and doctor. They had to be festive with the others, yet it was grim for both of them, more so for her than for him.

Dinner progressed uneventfully. The colonel's jokes and Viana's repeated toasts entertained the guests. Félix tried to get into the festive mood and managed to do so. He failed to notice—what a shame!—that the widow's countenance seemed increasingly saddened. His eyes sought Meneses's instead of hers, while Meneses's gaze was absorbed with Lívia.

When dinner was over, Viana suggested they retire to the garden to continue their colloquy. Meneses asked the colonel's daughter if she would first play a melody he had heard some days prior. Raquel agreed. The song was extremely melancholy, and Raquel played from her soul. Its tone influenced the mood. The silence was not merely from attentiveness, rather the woe of solitude.

For some of them this impression was more natural and spontaneous. The doctor, however, struggled with it, not only shaking off the strange influence, but feigning absolute lack of feeling.

Luís was before him, resting his elbows on Félix's knees. Félix was tousling his hair, and they were smiling at each other, as if they were the only two exempt from the general mood.

Then, amidst the absolute silence of the room, with only the solitary, pained notes Raquel's fingers drew from the piano, Lívia's young son posed the following naive question to the doctor:

— Why don't you marry my mother, sir?

Lívia shuddered. Raquel stopped playing and turned her head suddenly toward the group from where she had heard the voice. A few of them smiled at the little boy's innocent indiscretion, others observed the widow, no one noticed Raquel.

The colonel's daughter got up from the piano immediately. Viana once again suggested they take a turn in the garden. Everyone accepted the proposal and left the parlor. The sense of discomfort the boy's question had created soon dissipated—for some of them, but not all.

Lívia did not leave at once. At a short distance they noticed her absence, and Raquel offered to go after her.

Raquel found Lívia embracing and kissing her son. Although she was a devoted mother, there was no apparent reason for that outpouring of tenderness. Raquel halted, entirely perplexed.

The widow looked at her, holding the child close to her breast.

— What do you want? she asked.

Raquel did not answer. Little by little it dawned on her. She looked at Lívia for a long while, as if to extract an explanation by sheer force of will, the explanation she sensed in her heart. Finally, she seemed to have guessed at everything.

— You love him, then? she asked with trembling lips.

— I think I did love him, Lívia responded bowing her head sadly.

If Raquel's soul did not still rest within the bosom of chastity, the widow's false confession—for she was still in love with the doctor—may well have given birth to improper suspicions. But Raquel heard nothing more in those words than fearful, misunderstood love. Her eloquent response was to take Lívia in her arms.

Lívia held her tightly. It was the first time that chance had brought her a confidant. Her breast pounded, swollen with sighs. Two tears burst from her eyes, vanishing on Raquel's shoulder. The boy interrupted this sweet effusion. Lívia breathed heavily, kissing the girl tenderly.

— Let us go.

But Raquel did not move. Her eyes were on Lívia, her lips pursed and her arms limp. Lívia shook her shoulders gently.

— What's wrong?

— Nothing, Raquel sighed.

Lívia shivered. A flash of lightning traversed the shadows of her soul. She asked Raquel again, but it was in vain. Then she sensed all the energy of her nature gathering within, her cry dulled by anger.

— Oh! You love him too!

Raquel did not answer. If the widow had spoken to her tenderly, she probably would have confessed her feelings fully. But with Lívia's angry words, the poor young girl began to tremble.

— You love him too! was Lívia's hard, firm response.

Raquel bent over, her hands clasped, and murmured in a faltering voice.

— Forgive me!

A sarcastic smile broke from the widow's lips. Raquel repeated over and over the word forgive, but her rival's only answer was to take her by the arm, gesturing toward the door.

— Go to him! she exclaimed.

Lívia left the room furiously. Raquel, hurt by the violence of the widow's expression, followed her with her eyes until she reached the door. The eyes of the offended doe were not flaming with hatred at the angry lioness.

XVI
Raquel

Left on her own, Raquel threw herself on the divan, trembling, her eyes dry. She was bewildered after that intimate drama, but already sensing some terrible dénouement. She saw clearly Lívia was in love with the same man, and so intensely that she had surrendered to impulsive rage, very contrary to her usual gentle habits.

Raquel's thoughts did not go beyond that. Not all souls are able to confront great crises. A robust spirit is needed for these complex situations. Raquel was simply dumbfounded and defeated.

Their absence was noted in the garden. Viana left his guests and went back to the house.

— What are you doing here? he asked the colonel's daughter.

Raquel was dismayed at his presence, and even more so with the question. Finally, she gave him a halting, childish answer.

— I was thinking about something, she said.

— Where's Lívia? Viana asked, ignoring both the girl's

answer and the smile she had forced from her lips.

— I think she's upset. She's retired to her room.

— Is it something serious?

— I don't think so.

Viana paced the room twice and went back out to the garden, requesting that Raquel join them.

Félix, meanwhile, had gone around to the front garden. He had taken but a few steps when he saw the colonel's daughter leaning against the parlor door, gazing at the sky, perhaps asking God to reach out a hand so she could ascend. It was dusk, the hour of melancholy. Everything around took on the tawny, glowing color of late afternoon.

Félix walked cautiously toward the house, climbed up one flight of stairs, and surprised the young lady.

— You're very pretty posed like that, but we need to see you outside.

Raquel withdrew, without daring to utter a word. Félix reached out his hand to her, encouraging her to come down. Instead, the girl withdrew indoors. The doctor took one more step forward, but she, with a pleading gesture, spoke fretfully.

— For the love of God, leave!

Félix did not insist. He went back outdoors and walked toward the open garden to join the others. He tried in vain to deduce the cause of her entreaty. It was impossible to reconcile Raquel's behavior with their mutual familiarity and trust. The cause of that discrepancy must be grave. But what could it be?

The guests retired early. Meneses and Félix were the last to leave, side by side, each with their own thoughts, because Félix was thinking about Raquel's words, and Meneses, about the boy's question.

The colonel's daughter went downstairs to the garden. It was pitch dark. She sat down on a small bench and stayed there in sad meditation. The poor young woman was shaking with fear, uncertainty, and apprehension. She did not dare look Lívia in the eye. She was afraid of her. It was a childish fear, needless, and without reason, but nonetheless, it was fear, and there would be no quelling that timid, feeble soul.

Like a celestial blessing, her tears, hitherto restrained by the presence of strangers, began to flow freely. No one saw them because the night was so dark and her retreat so enclosed. Yet, the summer breeze, rustling the sundried leaves, perchance heard her sobbing, perchance carried it to the bosom of God. And there came, by divine intervention, sweet consolation to her solitary tears.

Lacking the courage to go back indoors, she decided to wait there for Viana's return from accompanying a guest home. She would then ask him to convey her back to her parents' home the following day. She had no difficulty choosing between their kindness and Lívia's hatred.

These were her thoughts when she heard some footfalls in the garden. She turned around; it was the widow.

— Oh! exclaimed Raquel, standing, shaking fearfully. For the love of God! I did you no harm!

Lívia approached Raquel, gently taking her hands, in spite of Raquel's efforts to free herself.

— What harm could you cause me, child? I'm at fault. It's I who begs your forgiveness because I was cruel and unfair, surrendering to the selfishness of my heart . . . Forgive me!

— I forgive you everything! Raquel answered.

They fell into each other's arms. Never before had two

rivals strengthened their friendship more sincerely than those two young women. Long minutes passed without a word from either one. Perhaps they were thinking, perhaps unable to overcome their shyness. Lívia was the first to break the silence.

— How did you come to love him? she asked.

— I don't know, Raquel answered innocently. My love was born without my paying it any mind. I don't even know if it was born. I think it was merely a transformation because I'd grown used to admiring him from the time I was small. Maybe it was that admiration that became love when I grew up.

— You haven't confided in him?

— Oh no, never!

— And he?

— I was aware he was fond of me. He would tease me, like when I was a child, nothing more.

— And you resigned yourself to fate?

— What else could I do, if not that? I've had some hope of late, on what it's founded, I couldn't say. It's perhaps circumstantial because we've had more occasion to meet. But, I was mistaken, I don't think I was born to be happy.

— Who knows? said the widow. Our hearts aren't always wise; you may find that later on someone will appear who you'll love just the same . . .

— Just the same? Raquel interrupted with surprise. Lívia took her by the hands.

— So, you don't believe in such a future?

—Oh! No! Call me childish, if you wish. You, madame, must know more than I do, naturally. But my heart tells me I could never love anyone else.

— No one else! the widow murmured bitterly. So, your

heart's entirely taken up with this silent, dreamy love? Don't say that. You'll love someone later on who will love you in return, and you'll be happy, I believe that. This first blooming of your heart will wilt, but you've plenty lifeblood there to make another flourish, perhaps even as beautiful, and certainly more fortunate. Otherwise, Raquel, ours would be an unjust God. Love is the law of life, the reason for all existence. To fill your soul only once, without anyone's ever drinking the divine liqueur, and return to the heavens without knowing happiness on earth, is neither for God to will nor for you to fear. You speak now through bitter lips, but wait for the acts of time, there's your true friend.

Raquel was meditating. It was the first time she had ever heard matters of the heart spoken of in that manner. The widow's language was both consoling and enlightening.

Lívia continued talking for a long while more, with neither prejudice nor restraint. She did not speak like a rival, more like a friend and mother. She did not even realize she was giving the girl arms to use against her. She would perhaps have spoken differently had she considered her own circumstances propitious but, since the two young women's situations were identical, she poured into Raquel's soul all the sentiment with which her own was filled. She was eloquent because she was sincere.

— Yes, said Raquel, when Lívia had finished, I understand everything you're telling me. You, madame, know how to love . . . and you still love him, don't you?

Lívia was silent.

— What harm is there in saying so? the maiden insisted.

— My tears, that's the harm. I'd never be able to explain

my sentiments to you, born inside me like weeds, poisoning my existence. Sentiments I've held for so long as the crowning moment of my life . . . I don't want to be tiresome, it's merely sorrow.

— But, what of him? Raquel ventured.

— Don't press me anymore. I can only tell you I loved him, that I may love him again . . .

— And that you still love him, her rival concluded.

Lívia was still for a few seconds, trying to read Raquel's countenance, notwithstanding the shadows in the night, to sense impressions traversing her soul.

— No! I no longer love him! said the widow, not without effort.

A long silence followed.

— And, if you loved him, Lívia finally said, what would you do?

— Nothing! answered Raquel resolutely.

— Really, nothing?

— I'd ask God to help me make him happy, and I believe He'd hear me.

— Are you capable of that? asked the widow, holding Raquel by the wrists and staring her straight in the eye.

— I would be, the maiden answered innocently.

Lívia did not say a word. If any trace of the emotion churning in her soul reached her face, the night disguised it from Raquel's view. The two young women remained pensive for some time. A strong gust of wind gave them a jolt. It was the sign of approaching rain, dark clouds began to fill the sky. They went back inside the house.

— You're finer than I am, said the widow as she and Raquel entered the parlor. I'm merely selfish, selfish and nothing more. Protect your pious flowers, one each for sacrifice, forgiveness, and love. They're rare, and that's the reason you're an angel.

That night was unusual for them both.

Raquel was more serene after the conversation in the garden, but what was to be the fate of the flower in her soul, a lily transformed into a wallflower, surviving on tears and thriving in silence? She had no appetite for battle. She lacked the appropriate combat weapons—the artfulness or the energy. Mainly, she lacked the desire to arouse a heart she knew was not hers.

But, did this heart perchance belong to Lívia? She thought not. And yet, the mystery, her rival's reticence, her indecisive words—everything seemed to veil a drama Raquel could neither understand nor divine.

Lívia's spirits were otherwise occupied. In her mind, the situation was clearer. She sensed Félix's love vanishing, and saw the emergence of a dangerous rival. She feared Raquel's lack of awareness. She was apprehensive that her innocent, blossoming soul might come to dominate Félix's rebellious spirit, and that would be catastrophic for her own hopes.

While these shadows occupied Lívia's soul, and her heartbeat raced, her conscience questioned the justice of placing any obstacle before the maiden, given that she may have won her fiancé's heart.

Lívia did not sleep the entire night. The following day, as soon as daylight crept into her bedroom, the widow got up, hastily donned her peignoir, and went to Raquel.

The colonel's daughter was in a deep sleep. She was resting after her prolonged ruminations. Lívia opened the curtain very gently, contemplating Raquel's serene, smiling face. Her eyes shut, and lips slightly parted, as if in her dreams she were whispering words of love. Raquel's wispy hair was like a halo surrounding her angelic head.

"No!" thought Lívia. "Love doesn't sleep so peacefully on days of sorrow and desperation. Child, you're unawares, imagining yourself soaring through heavenly realms, what do you know of the precipices of that voyage, of the gulfs of the heart?"

— Oh! You were here! Raquel exclaimed, waking up. Thankfully!

— Why?

— I dreamt I was dying, and I'd gone to heaven. It was a fine way to die, but still, I regretted leaving Earth. You woke up very early today.

— I wanted to go walking, said Lívia, opening the window, but it's already so warm out this morning.

Raquel looked at her, her swollen eyes and exhausted expression. She realized Lívia had not slept, and that she had been crying.

"Does she love him very much?" she asked herself.

XVII

Sacrifice

The two young women's situation required a resolution. Raquel was the first to make a full retreat from the battlefield. Her recovered health was an excellent excuse to return home.

Lívia understood her friend's intention when the latter told her about her decision. The sacrifice was so simple and touching that the widow could not resist her gracious impulse. She answered with a kiss. It was a kiss of admiration. Raquel believed it was in thanks, and smiled sadly.

It was agreed Raquel would leave the following Sunday, and the colonel was informed as much.

The little boy had made his comment just the day prior. The doctor had forgotten nothing of what had transpired. Raquel's aloofness continued to plague him, no less than the unfounded suspicion he cultivated regarding the widow. It was mid-December. The wedding date was imminent. Everything required a swift decision.

It was not long before the doctor discovered the sentiments the colonel's daughter nurtured for him. He caught her unawares, kissing a photograph in an album as she sat nearby the window. He approached her cautiously, glanced at the album and saw a photograph of himself.

The discovery made him smile. Would that be the reason for her recent alteration in behavior? If such were the case, she would already know about the affectionate ties between himself and the widow, perhaps even about the forthcoming wedding. The motive behind her return to her parent's home was possibly none other than that. No matter how lacking a man's spirit may be, it is rare man indeed who is not flattered by such affections, fearful and silent, born and thriving within the solitude of a soul. Félix's first impression was such egoism. It was followed by a better one—respectful admiration. He began to wonder about the beginning of that singular love. As he mulled over the previous days, he pieced together several sporadic episodes, apparently unrelated at the time, but now significant and eloquent. Her affection was not recent, it may have dated back to before her illness.

Saturday had arrived, the day preceding Raquel's departure. It was nighttime. Félix was at the widow's house. The two of them, plus Raquel—even Viana—seemed worried and sad. The doctor was looking at the colonel's daughter, oblivious to Lívia's eyes, which followed his, trying to read the feelings in his heart.

Raquel evaded the doctor's attentive gaze. She had occasion though—finding Félix off to the side—to hand him a book.

— Have you read this book yet? she asked.

— Let me see, said Félix, gesturing for her to sit down.

Raquel did not take a seat. Instead, she handed the doctor the book, looking at him intently.

Félix accepted it and glanced at the first page. He was leafing through distractedly when a small folded piece of paper dropped onto his knees. Raquel looked fearfully towards Lívia who, standing near the piano, was playing a few solitary notes, disregarding the others. Raquel gestured for him to be silent, and he withdrew, placing the note in his pocket.

"Nearly a child!" he was thinking as he made his way home after the tea.

When he arrived, he did not bother to remove his hat. He opened the letter in the parlor.

"In memory of your mother, don't be cruel! Lívia loves you very much. Don't make her die, for it would be a sin!"

Félix rubbed his eyes and reread the note.

There was no denying it. It was Raquel's handwriting, a plea on behalf of her rival. The doctor did not smile, he was astonished. The truth, seemingly unimaginable, was right before his eyes—sincere, eloquent, spontaneous. Was it really spontaneous? Félix asked himself the question and answered in the affirmative. He did not attribute such great influence to the widow, nor such great submissiveness to the maiden for one of them to have inspired the other to pen that letter. It was exactly what it appeared to be, an enormous sacrifice on the part of Raquel.

Félix was not an expansive man, but if Raquel had been with him just then, he might have fallen at her feet. To have suppressed her silent affection, perhaps her first, to beg for another woman's happiness, was rare altruism, and it surprised him.

Raquel's act had momentarily made him forget the widow, who was the subject of the missive he had just read. Raquel would not have avowed to her friend's sentiments so clearly if she were not entirely certain of their nature. How then to reconcile today's assertion with yesterday's suspicion? The very same Raquel had insinuated a different inclination on the part of the widow. Naturally, he had recognized the opposite. The idea of Lívia's redemption immediately dominated Félix's mind. His love existed with the same strength and vigor. Easily faded, it was no less easily brought back to life. The following day it seemed as if the cloud hanging over him for several days had dissipated.

He went to the widow's house. It was one o'clock in the afternoon. He was keen on meeting the colonel's daughter. He found her just as happy and mischievous as ever, or at least she seemed thus. An outsider's eyes would not view the inner, hidden pain gnawing away at her heart. There was modesty to her sorrow.

It was impossible for the doctor to conceal his state of mind. The young woman's touching generosity did Félix's heart good. He was heedful so as not to treat the widow in such a manner hurtful to the maiden. Nonetheless, he was so different than he had been up until then that the widow could not resist him, and that day was far less sorrowful than the others.

Luís's mischief acted as a chorus to Raquel's. The living room door was open. Luis went down the stairs leading from the living room to the garden, just as Lívia was fastening Raquel's bracelet. When the widow realized he was gone, she ran to the door. The boy was running towards the gate leading to the street. Lívia went down after him.

Raquel prepared to follow suit, but Félix took her by the hand. The girl trembled throughout. Her cheeks were burning and she stammered.

— Did you read my letter?

— I did, Félix answered, staring into her eyes—his own, filled with both sympathy and pity. I read it, but I don't know whether or not to believe what it says.

— It's the truth.

— But then you suppose? . . .

— That she loves you . . . I'm telling you.

— And that I love her too? he asked hesitatingly.

— That's . . . what I think, Raquel agreed, lowering her eyes.

Félix was quiet. Two or three minutes of silence transpired. Raquel contained her throbbing heart with difficulty. She would have preferred to have been miles away, but was strengthened by the thought of her friend. The doctor was the first to speak.

— How do you know she loves me?

— I just do, Raquel answered, smiling affectedly, and that's enough. And furthermore, no girl would ever write a man such a letter if she weren't completely sure of what she was saying. All I ask of you is this: destroy the letter. It has no value; still, I would much prefer you didn't keep it.

Lívia was approaching. They could hear the footsteps on the stone staircase. Raquel ran to the door, while Félix took his billfold from his pocket, and looked for Raquel's missive. At that very moment the colonel and his wife arrived. The two young women went down to greet them. Félix also went down, walking a few paces behind, his heart divided between his love for Lívia and his admiration for Raquel.

The young woman's parents dined in Laranjeiras. Lívia then accompanied the entire family back to the city. As she took her leave from the doctor, the colonel's daughter felt her strength giving way. She recovered herself though and, without looking at him, held out her hand, which the doctor respectfully clasped. As she turned around, a sigh escaped her bosom. Her last hopes were dashed.

XVIII

Renovation

Lívia was not to remain ignorant of Raquel's letter for long. Félix showed it to her the following day, yearning to discover how that conviction, so generously affirmed, had been born in the young woman's spirit.

— I told her everything, said the widow, when I thought all had died in your heart. She was sympathetic, and I now see her sentiment wasn't devoid of feeling. Poor Raquel!

— This letter's been a great consolation, Lívia, because I'd suffered cruel doubts in your regard . . . But what were your reasons for speaking to her?

Lívia hesitated for a few moments. Rather, she repressed her first instinct, which was to tell the doctor about Raquel's love and confession. It would have been in keeping with her character had she done so, but her fleeting consideration of the idea restrained the confession on her lips. Did she fear the knowledge of such a generous love would lead him away from her? Perhaps. The explanation she gave him was brief.

— I've told you, Lívia responded. I confided the reason for my sorrow on one occasion when she seemed particularly concerned for me. If I've done wrong, the fault is your own.

Félix did not insist. For his part, he left off any explanation for his recent aloofness. While the widow, who knew the reason, thought it best not to talk about it.

So oft vanished from the heavens, had the star of happiness finally reappeared forever? The case was doubtful, given their history, yet the widow's credulity outdistanced her experience. Félix's tenderness had never been more lively nor spontaneous, as if his heart were renewed. Raquel's sacrifice was not foreign to this turn of events, which had led to the rekindling of all the widow's hopes.

Joy flourished anew on the widow's countenance, and in her breast. She recalled only happiness, no grief. Any lingering sorrows were erased with time. The serenity of the early days was all that remained.

On one occasion, there appeared a passing cloud, in the form of Meneses, who still frequented the widow's home. Félix's manner in greeting the guest led her to believe there were still traces of bitterness in his heart. It was not difficult to extinguish them definitively. She innocently brought up all that had passed between herself and Meneses, and her gentle austerity in responding to his amorous declarations, and finally, the upstanding behavior of the young man himself.

Félix nodded his head.

— Do you censure me? the young woman asked.

— No, the doctor said, I pity you.

— My intention was good.

— It would be. But life's not composed of feelings. One

doesn't carry on as if living in a novel. Generous instincts are all very well and good, when there's no risk of danger. Who's sworn by that young man's honesty?

— Oh! Guess! . . . Do you want proof? He won't come back here.

— Why?

— I believe he's divined everything.

The doctor was pensive for some time. Twice he tried to speak, but restrained himself. Finally he did.

— There's no need to guess tomorrow's certainty. We'll be married the second week of January. The news will be made public immediately.

Félix awaited the widow's enthusiasm upon hearing this declaration. Lívia remained impassive, merely paled.

— You're right, said Félix after observing her a while, I've no longer the right. So often I've led you astray, your reticence is legitimate.

The following day the doctor made his request official in the presence of Viana, who embraced his future brother-in-law zealously.

— It had to end precisely in this manner, he said. I'd predicted this union and hoped for it for a long time. You were born for each other. You're both in the prime of life, there could be no better marriage. For my part, if necessary, I'll even give up the trip you'd promised me, sir. You don't recall? Not a problem. All I want is to see the both of you happy. I perceived at the outset there were goings-on, but I compliment you both on your skill. Embrace me again, doctor.

Félix endured the parasite's effusion. Lívia contemplated her fiancé with adoration. For both of them, the entire world had disappeared. Not the entire world, for Viana made a casual reference to Raquel, and this ill-timed memory saddened the young woman. She realized her joy was cause for her friend's sorrow and, now that her own happiness was nearly fulfilled, she felt a pinch of pious remorse.

Preparations for the wedding were underway. Lívia asked the doctor to eliminate all pomp, to spare Raquel's feelings. Publicity was to be kept to the bare minimum. Although she could not count on her brother, who took it upon himself to lend the marriage grandiose proportions.

He spread the news on Rua do Ouvidor, at the corner of Rua Direita. Ten minutes later, it had reached Rua da Quitanda. It traveled so fast that a quarter of an hour later it was the topic of conversation at the corner of Rua dos Ourives. One hour was enough for the news to have reached the entire length of our main thoroughfare. From there, it spread throughout the city.

Most people were astounded. No one believed Félix had decided to wed. There had been talk about the romance, it is true. Yet, aside from the trivial and fairly contained rumor, some did not credit the doctor with any intention beyond a dalliance, while others considered the relationship between him and the widow most certainly intimate, with no aspiration for legality whatsoever.

The conviction eventually became common knowledge. Moreirinha attributed the case to cerebral dysfunction on the part of the doctor. Doctor Luís Batista refrained from expressing his opinion. He was seemingly indifferent to the widow's marriage.

Upon hearing the news, Raquel was not surprised, rather sorrowful. She no longer held out any hope. Pain that does not come as a surprise is, nevertheless, no less painful. The news was brought to her by Meneses, who took it with philosophical resignation. His love for Lívia had been converted into a sort of religious adoration. He found in her all the qualities that could seduce a man such as himself. In addition, they shared a sympathy for living more in their imagination than in the real world. Lívia's refusal, rather than breaking the chains that attached him to her, had transformed them.

The same could not be said of Raquel, and this did not escape the attention of the young man, who questioned her ably, and guessed everything. Meneses nodded his head slowly, but did not say anything to her. He merely thought to himself that, if by chance Providence had determined things otherwise, both of them might have been happy.

Meneses rejected the idea of confiding in the colonel's daughter. Still, he spoke so much about the widow that Raquel's suspicions were aroused. In brief, knowing they were both suffering inside, their common unhappiness somehow linked them together. Since their relations were more cordial than familiar, neither one of them spoke with the effusion of their feelings. Though they guessed, which was plenty, and had pity for each other, which was almost everything.

XIX

The Doorway to Heaven

Two days preceding the wedding, at the colonel's invitation, Lívia went to dine with several close friends gathered at his home. Félix did not attend, although he had been invited forthwith. He had given in to a sentiment of delicacy, not wanting to humiliate the colonel's daughter with his presence, nor to trouble the widow's peace of mind in any way.

Lívia's first thought was to shirk the invitation, so as not to confront Raquel's suffering. But, Raquel's parents' entreaty was such that it was impossible for Lívia to refuse.

The two young women's greeting was emotional. The difference was that Raquel concealed her shaken spirits more effectively than did the widow. The maiden's poise redoubled her rival's admiration. Lívia understood Raquel's delicate intention, and thanked her the first opportunity she had.

— I know everything, Lívia added. I know about your letter, the key opening the doors to my renewed fortune.

I don't know if I'd have managed to be as heroic as you. Destiny separates us, let me kiss your hands.

Lívia gestured, accompanying her request, but Raquel refused to give in to the widow's wish.

— Be happy! she murmured.

Those were the last words between the two of them. When the widow left, they exchanged a kiss, which they could not refuse, and which on Raquel's part was far less spontaneous than on Lívia's. Lívia sensed this and forgave her sincerely.

Upon stepping into the carriage with her brother, the widow was disconsolate and sad. Her heart knew how to love, and the idea that her happiness came at the price of someone else's tears pained her deeply.

"Why," she thought, "does Providence have to insert this drop of bitterness into my overflowing cup? If I could at least ignore it . . . my joy wouldn't be hindered by remorse . . . Joy?" She continued following a new train of thought, "Would it really be joy? It's been almost a year since I've trusted my entire existence to this vague probability. The end is near, I don't know which bad fortune is driving me away. They say I'm beautiful, I should be content with being admired . . ."

At this moment the young woman was interrupted by a banal observation from Viana, whose feet served as an infallible thermometer. He announced an impending thunderstorm. Lívia looked at him silently, amazed at those for whom thunderstorms in the atmosphere are more important than thunderstorms in life. Viana probably would have thought the opposite had he been privy to his sister's worries.

When they arrived in Laranjeiras, they found Félix in the living room, conversing childishly with Lívia's son, who was asking him about the mechanism of the clock. Félix called on all the resources of his imagination to satisfy the boy's curiosity. Upon hearing a carriage stop, followed by the sound of footsteps in the garden, the doctor told the boy that his mommy had returned, and took the opportunity to tell the child he was going to marry her.

With this divulgence, the boy climbed onto the doctor's knees and asked him happily if he were telling the truth.

— Yes, it's true, Félix repeated.

— You're going to marry mommy, sir?

— I will, I already said so.

Right at that moment Lívia appeared in the doorway. The boy got down from Félix's knees and ran to embrace his mother.

— Is it true, mommy, you're going to marry Doctor Félix? he asked after she kissed him.

— Yes, it is, my son, she answered, entering and extending her hand to the doctor.

Félix's presence and Luís's joy altered the young woman's train of thought. Five minutes were enough for her to forget her own sorrow and the misfortune of her broken-hearted rival. Would Raquel be shedding tears just then, in the silence of her room, tears of longing? No one thought of that, neither the widow, whom she had so generously served, nor Félix who was the reason for those solitary woes.

Félix was more jovial than ever. He had lost all of his cold, polished manners. He had become expansive, garrulous, tender, almost puerile. His heart seemed to be filled with the present and the future. It was not merely the situation that explained this change, it was also the inconstancy of his soul.

The widow realized a poem of unutterable bliss had finally resurged in his soul. At one point, she was reminded of the same joyfulness as during the days preceding her first wedding, and she shuddered. It was not a lasting impression. Her second husband was not like her first, a man with no soul—rather, his soul was inanimate. But had love not already begun to reactivate it?

In forty-eight hours their destinies would be forever united. This grave, decisive act in a man's life the doctor was facing with the calm of a resolute soul, with neither concern for the responsibilities, nor apprehension of the consequences. He fancied domesticity as a city of peace and harmony. At its doors, he did not see the pale specter of doubt. Instead, his route was seemingly lined with flowers and lush foliage, not deathly but enlivening, inviting him to rest, finally, from his poorly lived life.

Lívia delighted in the rebirth of her lover. They were alone and were going to exchange their penultimate farewell kiss. Their last would be the following night. Her hands were on Félix's shoulders as their eyes sought to blend their souls in the same ray of light.

The heavens did not validate Viana's concerns. The clouds announcing the coming of the next storm had dispersed. There was no moonlight, but the night was clear. Perhaps some imaginative poet would have compared the lively stars sparkling above to the tongues of fire at that Pentecost of love.

— Swear to me yet once more that you love me! he

would say. It's sweetness to my soul to hear your confession.

— I swear by the heavens, by my son, by you, I swear I'll love you always. I loved you even when I knew you were indifferent to my affection, when you denied it, when you repaid me with disdain. Why would I not love you now that you're entirely mine . . . entirely, right?

— Are you in doubt?

— I don't know how to doubt, but fear, yes. I've already told you the reason. But today I'm not afraid. I believe I'm truly loved. No matter what my past grievances, I forgive you all now, now that you've opened the doorway to heaven.

— Oh! You're an angel!

— Good-bye!

— Good-bye! You love me very much, no?

— Very much!

And a chaste kiss, long and nearly divine, sealed this confession so oft repeated between them. Afterwards they clasped hands, and Félix departed.

The street was deserted, the silence, profound. Félix entered his house elated and pleased. He did not feel like sleeping. He turned to his books, but did not take advantage of the resource, his eyes merely skimming the pages, his spirit, absent from both time and space. He mused over his lover, designing their future.

With fatigue, drowsiness set in. Félix slept in the arms of angels.

It was eight o'clock when he woke up and opened the windows. The day was grim. There was a relentless drizzle that had begun with the first signs of dawn. What did he care of Nature's melancholy if his own soul was a source of overwhelming joy?

He sat down at his desk and spent two hours taking stock of his bachelor life, indifferently tearing up an enormous quantity of letters, reminders of extinct loves, or simply passing fancies. He swept out the temple wherein his heart's chosen one was to enter. When he reread some of these epistolary specimens—fallen leaves from seasons long-gone—his lips formed an ironic, yet serene smile, such was the transformation of his soul, now indifferent to past battles.

At ten o'clock he got up to go to lunch. He had just sat down at table when he was informed that he had a caller.

It was Doctor Luís Batista.

XX

A Mysterious Voice

Félix stopped abruptly at the door of the parlor. Luís Batista took two steps towards him.

—You've never opened your home to me, he said. My indiscretion is means of rectifying your oversight.

Was it a jest or gibe? Félix restricted himself to clasping Luís Batista's extended hand and inviting him to take a seat.

— They told me you were having your luncheon, Batista observed. I don't want to disturb you, by any means. Go right ahead, I'll stay here leafing through a book.

— I was just going to start, the doctor responded. If you'd like, we could take our luncheon together.

— No, if you'll allow me, since you're still a bachelor, I'll keep you company while you dine, then I'll delve into what brings me here.

Félix invited him in and the two sat down at the table. The first sentences they exchanged were sparse and cold, but the guest's natural manner won his host over.

— It's true, said Batista, I've heard you're getting married . . .

— Tomorrow.

— I'm therefore observing the penultimate luncheon of your bachelorhood. There are still plenty of folks who don't believe it. I believe you, sir, had the reputation of the inveterate bachelor and, according to rule, an inveterate bachelor is a groom in waiting. I too was like that. Nonetheless . . . marriage is good, albeit entailing a few inconveniences, like everything else in this world. Still, by and large, good, on the one condition—that we accept it as it should be . . .

— Somewhat free? said Félix, smiling.

— I don't know whether somewhat or very much, it's a question of temperament. What is essential is the freedom. That's how I understand marriage, and how I practice it. I'm a miserable sinner, I confess, but at least I have the merit of not being hypocritical, and just now . . .

— Just now? Félix repeated, after a few moments of silence.

— I'm not sure I should tell you this, after all you, sir, are still a neophyte. Naturally you'll be put off, curse me . . . But, in brief, it's imperative I tell you everything, since it has to do with the reason I've come.

Batista accepted the cup of coffee the doctor offered him. Then, in an insolent, flip tone, he referred to his love affair of the past few days. It involved a capricious, oft courted woman. His triumph was thus twice glorious. As a beauty, he challenged the doctor himself to resist her after a half hour's conversation. Other more gorgeous women might be found, but this one knew how to use her mysterious enchantment to entice even the most rebellious will.

— When she stares at me with her large eyes, Luís Batista continued picturesquely, it's as if molten lead were poured into my veins.

His entire description was in these terms—jovial and sensual. He spoke for twenty minutes with the enthusiasm fitting his circumstance. Félix listened to his guest's story patiently, failing to grasp what it might have to do with the request he was going to put forth. He was irritated inside. The doctor in his long years of bachelorhood had been neither chaste nor cautious, but the atmosphere of the engagement had begun to refresh his spirit, and that sort of confidence, on that occasion, seemed in every aspect extravagant.

I'm not unaware, said Luís Batista when he had concluded his treatise on love, I'm not unaware that an amorous adventure, on the eve of the engagement ceremony produces the same effect as an Offenbach[34] aria in the middle of a Weber[35] melody. But, my fine fellow, to each his own. It's the law of human nature. Life's but an *opera buffa*[36] with intervals of serious music. You, sir, are experiencing an interval. Enjoy your Weber until the curtain lifts on your Offenbach. I'm sure you'll come sing with me and assure you, you'll find a good partner.

This said, Luís Batista swallowed the last of his coffee, now gone cold, relit his cigar, and leaned back in his chair. Félix had time to regain his composure, which had been disconcerted by Batista's concluding comments.

So, said Félix, what's the relation between this adventure and what you've come to ask me?

Everything, Batista responded. If there were none, I wouldn't be here asking you any favors. You know how capricious a lover can be; nor would you deny that her every wish is the command of her chosen knight.

Félix gestured in agreement.

— Well then, Batista continued. Here's the situation. She's extremely capricious, even beyond capricious, she loves *objets d'art*. Several days ago I found her in a state. I asked what was wrong, but she was disinclined to tell me anything. As the conversation progressed, she mentioned two or three times an engraving she'd spotted on Rua do Ouvidor, but which the owner had already sold when she returned to buy it. It was the most orthodox theme possible: the Israelite Bathsheba[37] in her bath with King David[38] spying on her from his terrace. Doesn't that seem gay? I believe the engraving was indeed quite fine, but for the person in question, it was especially valuable. Bathsheba's features were identical to her own. A pretty, young woman's vanity. She was so disconsolate as she told me this, it was easy to perceive there was no other cause for the state I'd found her in.

— And then?

— I did what anyone else would have. She had to have a copy of that engraving at all costs. I looked for it, but to no avail. I spent two long days researching, and when I went back to her house there was nothing left for me to do but dash her last hopes. She held my hands affectionately and thanked me for my efforts, telling me it was yet one more proof of my love for her. Still, she ended all of this with a sigh. I won't venture to tell you, sir, what a sigh means under these circumstances. That sigh was her resolve to obtain what she wants.

— It seems so, said Félix, who had already guessed the end of the story.

— You'd say, Batista continued, I should've taken advantage of the packet-boat that left yesterday and had the engraving sent from Europe. I'd have no reservations about doing that, and she'd willingly wait. But who's to say my love will outlast the ship's return? Then I came up with the perfect solution.

— Ah!

— I went back to the store where she'd seen the print and asked the owner who'd bought it. After scrutinizing his memory, he told me it was you, sir. At first I hesitated, not wanting to be inopportune. My request wouldn't be indiscreet on any other occasion, but since you're on the verge of entering a moral state, begging you to help me dry the tears of a beautiful sinner, goes beyond indiscretion, it's rash. I hesitated, but the voice of reason was weaker than that of sin. Sin won the day.

Luís Batista was then quiet, awaiting the doctor's response. There was a long silence. They got up from the table and went to the parlor, and Félix still offered no response. Luís Batista was the first to take up the topic.

— Are you unable to satisfy my request?

— I've been asking myself if I'm justified, as I join the ranks of matrimony, to aid a deserting comrade, Félix responded jovially.

Luís Batista was singularly talkative that day. The doctor's simple observation served as a pretext to a long discourse on the matrimonial state. It was twelve o'clock noon. Félix had long tired of both the visit and the discussion. He took advantage of a pause.

— In sum, you want the engraving very much?

— I'd like you to cede it.

— I'll make you an offer.

— I don't want to set you back in any way, said Batista, so you must allow me to give you a wedding gift.

Félix did not answer. He went to get the engraving in question and returned with it. Luís Batista could not contain his surprised cry. The painting's Bathsheba, he said, was the spitting image of his lady. The lady was perhaps even more beautiful than the copy.

At that precise moment, a letter was brought to the doctor, delivered by post. Félix opened it distractedly, but as soon as he had read its contents, he went very pale and reached for a chair for support. He brought the paper closer to his eyes, his hands trembling, as he bit his lips drawing blood. Luís Batista approached him quickly and asked what was wrong.

— Nothing, said the doctor, just dizziness, please excuse me, I must withdraw.

The guest bowed, smiled, and departed.

Félix shut himself inside his bedchamber. What went on there, no one in the household discovered. Every once in a while there was some noise, but muffled, and some exclamation or another, vague and incoherent. It was four o'clock when the doctor emerged into the parlor.

The weather had improved. The sun had reappeared between the two clouds, beating down on the drenched trees and dripping rooftops. One might say nature had created a distinct contrast from that morning, because now, the afternoon smiled joyfully, while the man showed signs of an interior storm. His eyes were red, his mouth grimaced, his hair disheveled. He stepped out unsteadily.

Occasionally he strove for courage, looking as if breathing itself were an effort. A servant, to whom he had given orders, noticed his master's state and asked if he had fallen ill. Félix answered no, brusquely. The slave bowed his head and left.

Félix then wrote a letter addressed to the widow. Afterwards, he dressed. It was not long before a carriage stopped at the door. He stepped in and asked to be taken into town.

XXI

Final *Coup*

It was already evening when the letter reached the widow's hands. Viana had gone out to the grounds whilst his sister divided her attention between her son's pranks and her own thoughts. The boy's presence filled the entire parlor, although his mischief was not tiresome. Lívia watched over him with more than just a mother's eyes for she saw him as the golden tie between ruined and realized dreams. Those were her thoughts when the mammy came in with Félix's letter. She handed it to her and left.

Lívia trembled. The address revealed the feverish state of the hand that wrote it. She opened the letter rapidly and read it.

When Luís, running in circles, stopped near his mother, he found her staring at the floor, shaking and pale. He called to her, uselessly. He grabbed her hands and the young woman seemed to awaken from a lethargic trance.

— What's wrong mommy? the boy asked, tearfully caressing her.

Lívia did not answer at first. The child's voice finally

brought her back to reality. She looked around the room vaguely and, as if she were regaining consciousness little by little, she turned her eyes to the fatal letter. She was still holding it, and read it once more anxiously. She got up suddenly, taking few steps, then falling once again into the chair. The boy ran to the door fearfully. His uncle entered at that moment.

— What's going on? said Viana, noting the child's frightened expression, and the distressed expression on his sister's face.

Lívia handed him the letter.

"Lívia.

What I'm going to do lacks dignity, I know that. It is even more cruel than undignified. Our marriage is irrevocably impossible. You are neither directly nor indirectly responsible for my decision. This letter, my condemnation, will be your ultimate defense. Farewell.

Félix"

When Viana finished reading this strange, mysterious document, he turned as pale as his sister. He understood nothing. Nonetheless, he was indignant with Félix's behavior. He stifled his anger in an attempt to ward off the widow's fury. They looked at each other silently for a few moments. The boy had approached and was holding on to his mother's hand, looking up at his uncle as if he were expecting some sort of explanation.

— He's refused, Viana finally said, and offers us no explanation of his behavior. The act is so undignified, you shouldn't be devastated. When a man reveals such sad documentation of his loyalty, I think the woman who loves him should thank God she hasn't followed him to the altar. I hope you'll see it as I do . . .

Viana was unable to finish. The widow's tears, held back for so long, finally burst forth, impetuously and bitterly. Her pain, for having been initially so contained, became violent and explosive—but the young woman's body, beaten down with so much emotion, collapsed.

It was nighttime when she revived. She found herself in her own bed, with her brother and a doctor at her bedside.

The doctor spoke to her and she responded, unaware of what she said or heard. She had a terrible fever, but the doctor expected the medicine he had administered to take effect by the next day.

Viana was alone with his sister and tried to distract her from the events of the afternoon, a futile task since the widow was not thinking about them. Her vague stare indicated her spirit still held no light. She occasionally furrowed her brows and stared into space as if she were trying to remember. Once she gazed around the room as if looking for someone. Félix's absence filled her soul entirely.

She released a muted scream and burst into tears.

Her brother rushed to her side, with gentle words and advice, telling her not all was lost, the harm could be mended. Lívia did not believe in his vain consolation, she had given in to her desperation. Smothered in sobs, soaked with tears, she cried out in anguish and struggled convulsively in her bed.

Viana feared her grave state and sent for the doctor. When he arrived, the patient had already calmed down. But along with the tears, she had lost her reason. Her delirium lasted throughout the night and into the following morning. That afternoon, the fever subsided slightly and the patient slept.

Finally, the next day, when weariness had replaced her
frenzy, the young woman was able to reflect on her recent
misfortune. To no avail, she asked herself the reason for
her fiancé's sudden rift, to no avail. There must be some
mystery, some apparently legitimate reason, because the
widow's heart could tell her nothing that compromised
the doctor's loyalty.

Her brother told her he had been to the doctor's house,
but had not found him. Nor would anyone reveal his
whereabouts. Now, upon reflection, Viana was determined
to go to him in demand of an explanation.

Lívia disapproved of his decision.

— But, said Viana, we can't leave things as they are.

— We can, interrupted the widow. As long as I'm ill,
the explanation will seem natural to everyone. When I'm
on my feet again, I'll say I'm the one who broke it off.
You've always thought me peculiar, others probably do as
well. The final explanation couldn't be better.

— But what about his explanation . . .

— His isn't necessary.

Upon learning of Lívia's illness, Raquel went to spend
a few days with her. Under those circumstances, their
meeting was deeply sorrowful. At first, the widow did not
confide the true cause of her illness, but her restraint was
not long lasting because Raquel was concerned over Félix's
absence. Lívia thought it wise to tell her everything. For the
second time, the two young women found in each other's
arms, not consolation, for there is no such thing for such
recent disillusion, but momentary respite for their hearts.

Lívia began to convalesce from the blow of the fatal
letter. Raquel became her dedicated nurse and continued

to be the same affectionate friend she always had been. The widow could hardly believe her own restored health. In her opinion, it was but an impression, which reality would soon dismantle.

Ten days after the rupture with Félix, Meneses appeared in Laranjeiras. He had heard some talk regarding the doctor's marriage. He knew it had not come to pass, although the true reason was, as yet, unexposed. He had, however, become aware of Lívia's illness and to this he attributed the postponement of the wedding.

The young lady released a sigh upon seeing him come forth. It was not regret, perhaps self-pity, unable to accept this heart, trustful and less harsh than the other.

But if their alliance, which was not to be, was by then impossible—even though it made sense—Meneses's visit was auspicious, providing Lívia with a confidant for her misfortune. That was her first impulse, her second stemmed not from pride, but from modesty. In her heart, she was ashamed to admit her error before the man she had once rejected.

The situation was not easily hidden from Meneses's eyes. Her fiancé's absence was inexplicable. Meneses suspected the truth and Raquel confirmed it. Her revelation of the secret was yet one more sacrifice. She asked him to intervene, to facilitate the widow and the doctor's reconciliation.

— I'm asking you something very difficult, she concluded, alluding to Meneses's unrequited love, but it's a good deed.

— It is a good deed, and it is not difficult, he replied, regarding her fixedly. Raquel lowered her eyes severely. An attentive spectator might have concluded, perhaps, that his scar was not far from healing; while hers, on the contrary, continued to bleed.

Meneses agreed to make an attempt. He acknowledged Félix's behavior was mysterious. However, he was convinced of his ability to ascertain the wherefore and was confident he could remove it. He had managed to discover the doctor had taken refuge in Tijuca. Just as he was on the verge of seeking him out, upon reflection he hesitated and changed his mind.

A new crisis was needed to spur him on. The widow had a relapse, unable to withstand the long vigils and wakeful nights. This time the illness was less violent, but more tenacious. The fever was not intense, but there was no relief. The attending doctor did not believe she was in danger. He recommended extreme care in her treatment and absolute repose for her spirits.

Meneses did not hesitate. He went to Tijuca.

XXII

The Letter

When Meneses arrived in Tijuca, it was four o'clock in the afternoon. Félix's house was off the main road. The gate was ajar, so Meneses quickly traversed the space between the road and the house and rapped at the door. A servant boy came to open the door. Meneses entered rapidly.

— Where's doctor Félix?

— The doctor isn't talking to anyone, the boy responded, holding the key in such a manner as to encourage Meneses to take his leave.

— He must speak to me, Meneses insisted resolutely.

The young man's decisive tone unnerved the boy, whose spirit, so accustomed to obedience, was scarcely able to recognize obligation. The two went down a hallway, reaching another doorway. Before giving him entrance, the boy admonished Meneses to wait outside. The recommendation was wasted breath because, as soon as the boy opened the door, Meneses rushed in behind him.

It was a small office with four windows, filled with light. Near one of them there was an extended hammock.

Therein was a man carelessly reclined with a book in his hands.

It was Félix.

Félix lifted his head, met Meneses's eyes and paled. Meneses did not take another step. They remained so for several moments, looking at one another. Finally, the doctor dismissed the servant and the two were alone.

The silence went on even longer. On Félix's part, it stemmed from confusion; on Meneses's, disappointment. Throughout his ride over he had imagined what state Félix would be in, undoubtedly prostrate from some terrible pain, instead he found him reading peacefully. He wanted to seize the book, to discover the full extent of his disillusion, but the doctor stashed it hastily.

— You've failed to comply with the general household instructions I've issued, Félix finally said, I can only believe you're compelled by a very strong reason.

— I was, but the reason no longer holds, I'm returning to town.

As he said this, he put his hat on, heading toward the door. He stopped short, walked back over to the hammock and delivered these words curtly:

— Do you realize what you've done?

— Yes, Félix answered. I did what I had to. But, first things first, have you come on your own accord or have you been sent by . . .

— I've come because it's my duty to absolve you from your guilt and her from death.

— Death! exclaimed Félix, leaping up.

The terror that appeared on his face impressed his friend. Meneses suspected not all was lost. They both sat down, and Meneses recounted the events I have narrated in the previous chapter. Félix listened to the account with the rapt attention that could only come from love. Meneses concluded, painting the situation in all the appropriate colors, the baseness of Félix's behavior, the widow's disgrace, and the remorse that would haunt Félix, even if that sad episode had no fatal consequences.

Félix appeared to be deeply moved, by both the narrative and his friend's concerns.

— You're right, he said, when Meneses was through talking. My behavior was cowardly. She still loves me . . . And she's forgiven me, is that right? Yes, she must forgive me . . . Poor Lívia! If you knew how she's suffered over me . . . !

Meneses, satisfied, told him it was essential that he return to the city. As he was speaking, however, Félix's face changed expressions. The doctor responded summarily.

— No! What's done is done. It's no longer possible to recant.

— Not possible! shouted Meneses.

— Not possible, Félix repeated placidly.

Meneses got up impatiently and began to pace. The doctor's calm caused him more pain than anger. He sensed there must be some grave reason for Félix to have categorically refused all attempts at reconciliation. Meneses wanted to know what it was, yet trembled at the thought of asking.

Meanwhile, the doctor remained seated, almost as calmly as he had been when Meneses entered his study.

His calm was not feigned, it had been going on for several days, in the wake of others—the first days—which had been harrowingly turbulent.

A man cannot hide from himself, and the worst pain

inflicted on a pusillanimous heart is to realize it is so. When Félix arrived in Tijuca the initial commotion had passed. His spirit, weak by nature, and beaten by the magnitude of the blow, did not find the relief it sought in solitude. Days and days of struggle and fever followed during which, to strengthen his spirits, he read and reread the mysterious letter he had brought with him. That medicine was but poison for his ulcerous soul. It only reminded him of his lost happiness.

This was what ailed his heart. His conscience also suffered because society, which he had not considered initially, now seemed to be passing ruthless judgment, demanding he justify the inexplicable harm. At times, he regretted the act. At others, he did not, but condemned his own precipitation and irrationality. Never before had the inconstancy of his spirit been so sadly revealed.

With time, his conscience gradually quelled the voices and, with time and distance, and his inconstant character, his heart calmed down. That man, who only days before had wept desperately, now exhibited not a trace of those tears. His love for the widow had not been stifled. But, his vehement passion had seemingly been replaced by mere placid, remote memories. This change was brought about in part through his own efforts, through his having sought refuge in oblivion. Still, this was entirely in keeping with his instincts.

Thus were the circumstances in which Meneses found him. The latter's presence revived the doctor's memory of his recent amorous crisis. The impression was severe, but not long lasting—a lake, briefly rippled by the blast, had regained its natural serenity.

Meneses paced back and forth, glancing occasionally at the doctor. It was repugnant to his spirit that Félix had relied on extraordinary means to extricate himself from a difficult situation, a situation moreover that ran contrary to his heartfelt belief. Surely, there must have been some reason, which Meneses judged to be very grave, and which he wanted to discover at all costs. His efforts converged toward this end.

Entreated by Meneses, Félix alluded to the letter he had received, but refused to show it.

— It contains a secret, he said, which prevents me from showing it to anyone. Lívia's entitled to my respect and, furthermore, I still love her.

These last words were said somewhat emotionally. Meneses did not give up hope of winning him over. His eloquence was in his sincerity. One could say he spoke with his heart on his sleeve. Félix's spirit gradually succumbed to the enchantment, as he himself recalled the joyful hours of the past and his ardent hopes for the future. His heart beat more quickly and his imagination nourished the rest. The letter, however, the fatal letter returned quickly to his mind, and his face fell before the insurmountable obstacle.

Exhausted from the struggle, Meneses decided to return to the city.

— I don't know what the others will think, he said, but I take with me the suspicion you've never loved her, and this piercing break was your means to preserve your freedom.

Upon hearing these words, Félix barely contained an angry gesture. Meneses's calm allowed him to regain his composure.

— You're right, he said after a while. I want at least one

person to recognize my innocence and dignity. Do you give me your word of honor you won't reveal anything I'm going to read you?

— I do.

Félix went to get his billfold, removed the letter and handed it to Meneses.

Meneses began to read.

"Miserable young man! You are loved like your predecessor. You will be humiliated just as he was. After a few months you will need Simone of Cyrene[39] to help you carry the cross, just like he did, which is why he went to a better place. If there is still time, back out!"

The letter was not signed.

Meneses was astonished, but it was the work of just a few seconds, very few. His generous nature was appalled at the idea of accepting that revelation.

— It's impossible, he said.

Félix lifted his head, which was resting between his hands, and retorted.

— That's your conviction, I only wish it were mine. But do you have anyone to bear witness against what's written?

— I don't know, Meneses responded heatedly, but I'm following my heart. It disgusts me to imagine this poor young woman . . . It's impossible! Furthermore, it's an anonymous letter!

— Sign the letter with whatever name you choose, it neither adds nor subtracts from its worth, if the revelation is true.

— Who says it's true?

— Who says it isn't? The doubt is enough to justify what I've done. It was not only misgivings over the future that urged me on. It was, above all, knowledge of the past. Her betrayal, if there was betrayal, should cause no pain to the husband who's departed, but for her new husband, the idea of her previous disloyalty destroys the foundations of any trust, crucial to happiness. I don't know what you'd have done in my case. I was compelled by both heart and mind.

Meneses listened to his friend attentively. When he finished:

— I believe you're sincere, he said. I understand you've suffered.

— So much!

— But will you consider an idea? Who'd have written the letter? Surely it wasn't a friend. Had it been, if he were concerned over your behavior, he would have spoken to you in person. Nor was it a disinterested party. So what's left is an enemy, either yours or hers.

— Hers?

— Or someone who'd stand to gain, you decide.

Félix thought for a moment.

— Enemies, I don't know that she had any; to gain . . . by which means?

— She's wealthy . . . perhaps some suitor . . .

— There were none.

Meneses did not relinquish his hypothesis. The more he thought about the revelation in the letter, the more his heart cried out against it. As far as he was concerned, Lívia's innocence was as clear as daylight. Félix sensed Meneses's conviction, and regretted he could not feel it with the same intensity and depth.

It was long past nightfall. Meneses said he would only return to the city the following day.

Félix understood his friend had not lost hope of con-
verting him and, far from irritated, he was thankful for
his intention. He had spoken openly of his love for the
first time, and he did so with abundance and sincerity.
He did not even recall that Meneses too had been in love
with the widow.

They talked about the letter over and over again.
Meneses asked the doctor under what circumstances he
had received it. Félix referred to Luís Batista's visit, the
reason he had been there, and their conversation up until
the letter had been delivered.

The oddness of Luís Batista's visit was not lost on
Meneses.

— Was this man in the habit of calling on you?

— Never.

— Were you among his friends?

— We had more reason to be enemies than anything
else.

Meneses hesitated, not daring to espouse his suspicion.
But the doctor's soul was ripe for it. Meneses's questions
alone planted the seed, which soon sprouted roots and
grew.

— So, you think he . . . ? the doctor ventured.

— I don't know. But don't you find the whole tale of
the engraving odd?

Félix thought for some time. As when someone's eyes
grow gradually accustomed to darkness, distinguishing
objects little by little, the doctor's spirit began to recall and
scrutinize all the events of that fatal morning. What he had
not seen at first now seemed clear and evident. Luís Batista's
suave, jovial tone, his strange verbosity, the amorous

episodes so offhandedly recounted to a man who was not his natural confidant. All of this joined to the humiliation Luís Batista had experienced when the widow closed her house to him—in sum, his ill repute—were more than enough evidence to find his visit unnatural. And yet, how to deduce from this the letter's authorship?

Meneses handily solved the mystery.

— If you were to discredit the letter, he said, the last person you would think of would be Luís Batista, because no one ever ill-treats a man of whom he's asking a favor.

Félix accepted the explanation. And yet what finally convinced him was something he had forgotten till then, but which was now decisive. The doctor rose quickly from his chair, took a few steps around the room, and stopped in front of Meneses.

— It's true, he said. He did it, it's certain! When I read the letter I was furious. He approached me. I asked him to leave me alone. He obeyed, but with a slight smile, which at the time seemed like savage indifference, but which I now realize was triumphant, his lips quivered. He did it! Oh! I can feel it.

Reader, let us understand each other. I'm the one telling this story, and can assure the letter was indeed from Luís Batista. However, the doctor's conviction—sincere, certainly—was less solid and thoughtful than befitted the state of affairs. His soul had allowed itself to savor a new suspicion, which the circumstances favored and justified.

When Meneses saw most of his task had been accomplished, there was no further need to mention Lívia. The doctor's pallor had vanished. By then he was only love and hate, contrition and revenge. They slept poorly that night, and when dawn invited them to arise, Félix was completely transformed. He was dying to get down on his knees before the widow and make a full confession of his indignity. That is what he called it; he would have called it something else, if events were to give him cause for further doubt.

They rushed their journey. Meneses was pleased with the outcome of his mission. He too had deplored the disaster, but was certain that everything would end as it should. A thousand rose-colored ideas filled Félix's mind as they headed swiftly towards the city.

XXIII

Farewell

As soon as they arrived back in town, Félix took leave of Meneses and went to Laranjeiras. He was trembling and hesitant. For the first time that day, he remembered the widow's illness. He feared he might be too late. He was not. The windows were open. He entered the garden, climbed the stairs, his eyes lowered. When he looked up, Raquel was before him.

Even though Raquel possessed a heart less than philosophical, and she was now resigned—as was Meneses—she did not meet the doctor without some inner turmoil. She had him come inside and then went to see the nurse.

When Lívia found out Félix was there, she smiled sadly and closed her eyes. As she opened them, she found her good friend Raquel waiting at the foot of the bed. Her eyes were not teary, just covered in a serene melancholic veil.

— Thank him for me, Raquel, and tell him he'll see me when I can leave here.

Félix received the message and felt its coldness, in spite of the sweet voice in which it was relayed. Nevertheless, it was a great deal, the reconciliation would not be long delayed.

Lívia's convalescence was faster than could be expected. Félix took advantage of the interval to make amends with Viana, who found within himself enough mercy to pardon the guilty party. The doctor's submissiveness was flattering, and his remorse seemed to be what it truly was—sincere. It would have been natural for him to ask Félix for an explanation for the breach, although Viana thought it judicious to remain quiet. His prevailing desire was the reparation of the damage.

Lívia finally agreed to see the doctor. She was in the parlor, wrapped in a white robe, with traces of the pallor from her illness still lingering. Under the circumstances of their reunion, she could not have been any better disposed. The young woman's aura was not happy, nor was it severe. Félix walked slowly toward her, at once timid and fascinated. Once again, as always, he sensed her dominance over his spirit.

When Félix confessed his complete repentance to her and begged her forgiveness for his errors, Lívia heard him with great serenity, and answered affectionately.

— I won't deny you the pardon you ask of me. That would be to doubt your regret, and I believe you're sincere. I could, perhaps, ask that you tell me what led you . . .

— It's such a sad confession, Félix interrupted.

— Then I'll not ask it of you. But shall you hear me out?

Félix bowed his head.

— I believe you're regretful, and I don't doubt your love, in spite of everything that's transpired. That should satisfy you. By way of destiny or nature, we weren't made for each other. Our marriage would be a mere ceremony. Beyond that, it would be our misfortune. It's better to dream of the happiness we might have had then to mourn that which we've lost.

Félix listened, disheartened and weary, to the young woman's words. He ventured neither a response, nor a question, but from his silence, she understood the sincerity of his anguish and regret.

— Even if this pains you, she continued, you can see I'm not at fault. I accept this situation, not of my doing, nor of yours, but a situation—as I was saying—created by destiny or nature. This is the best solution at this point.

—No it's not, he interrupted impetuously, no it's not because we'll both lose, and there's nothing to prevent us from deciding otherwise. I don't think you doubt my love. Nonetheless, I'm telling you, you don't understand it, not its value. I wouldn't be able, under the circumstances we find ourselves, to propose a rift that . . .

The young woman's smile as she listened cut him off at that point. He realized, it reminded him—how easily he had forgotten everything—it reminded him it was not his place to mention a breach. He murmured.

— I've no right to talk like this, and I see I deserve to be punished . . .

— It's not punishment, the widow cut him off, it's necessity. If there's any consolation in this, our last meeting, know that I love you as much as ever before, and that my own suffering will be even greater than yours. The marriage is now impossible. I have no idea what made you write that letter, but I guess it was some further doubt in my regard. If we were to marry, would there be no end?

— Yes! because I now believe and see that you've suffered for me. To have doubted your love is to have lost my mind. Moreover, Félix continued, while Lívia shook her head sadly—we'll live for each other only, we'll close off our house from the eyes of strangers . . .

— Even so, your dark moods will hound you, Félix. Your spirit breeds clouds, so the sky is never entirely clear. Doubts will follow wherever we find ourselves, because they live eternally in your heart. Believe me, let us love from afar, let us be for each other the luminous traces of our past. They'll last through time, gild and warm the mists of our old age.

Lívia pronounced these last words in a tremulous voice, a tear rolling down her pale face.

— Why should we separate, now that we are at heaven's door? Félix asked. I've no place to demand the joy I've repelled so many times, but if you could enter my soul you would see my errors, as enormous as they are—and they are—they have been driven by love. In the end, I've always given in to the cries of my conscious. Your finest act would be to forgive me by forgetting, and the only way to forget would be to revisit our hopes.

— I'll pardon everything, I've forgotten everything. the past is erased, and I harbor no ill will. What can't be erased is the future.

Félix wrung his hands. His desperation was obvious. The widow could hardly bear to face him. There followed a long silence, interrupted by Luís's arrival. The boy put an end to the interview. Félix still lingered, looking at the young woman for a long time, but read in her face her unshakeable determination. He got up to take his leave.

— Don't make mommy cry, said Luís, putting his little arms around her neck.

Félix walked out slowly, his eyes clouded, his spirit dark, his steps unsteady and, with great difficulty, he went out the door, now closed to him forever.

XXIV
Today

Ten years have passed since the events recounted in this book, long and dull for some, light and gladsome for others, which is the general law of our miserable human society.

Light and gladsome for Raquel and Meneses, whom I now have the pleasure to introduce to my readers as married, and lovers to this day. Devotion brought them together, their unity brought them love and fortune.

Little by little, Raquel's first love faded, and the young woman's heart found no better convalescence than to espouse her caretaker. If anyone had told her so when she was suffering over her love for the doctor, she would have shrugged her shoulders disdainfully, and with reason. Where to find a better proverb than the Japanese refrain— the night falls, filled with the following day. Raquel could not guess at the dawn born in the bosom of her night, but her belief now is that, in all of time, there could have been none more beautiful.

The colonel and Dona Matilde, within a few months

of each other, carried their rare, sweet union into eternity.

Lívia entered her autumn years peacefully. To this day, she has not forgotten her chosen one and, with the passing of years, she has spiritualized and sanctified her memories. Félix's errors are forgotten. The luminous trace she described in their last meeting is all that remains.

Back when monasteries played their role in novels—as the hero's refuge, at least—the widow would have ended her days in a cloister. Her solitary cell would be the natural ending to her life and, since profane eyes would never penetrate that sacred precinct, we would leave her there, alone and quiet, learning to love God and to forget man.

But the novel is secular, and heroes who need solitude must find it amidst the madding crowd. Lívia knew how to remove herself from society. No one ever saw her again at the theater, on the boulevard, or at gatherings. Her callers were few and intimate. Among those who had once known her, many had forgotten her. Some would not recognize her now.

Time might have revered her beauty, except for the catastrophe that darkened her life. Her sweet, serene face is already showing signs of imminent decline. The few who call do not notice, because her soul has not lost its charm. To this day she is the same lovable enchantress of former years. She herself, though, sees the flower wilting, and knows, before long, windy nights will scatter it across the floor. Still, just as her beauty never awakened vanity, her decay does not inspire terror.

To console her in her old age she has her son, upon whose education she concentrates all her strength. Luís has his mother's graces, slightly modified by manly touches.

He is only fifteen, but since he inherited his mother's austere manner, and a bit, a very small amount of her imagination, he seems less an adolescent, and more a man.

Félix would not be one to enter a cloister. If the painful impression of the events you readers have followed left him deeply worn, it soon faded. His love was extinguished like a lamp run dry of oil. It was the young woman's company that had nurtured the flames. When she disappeared, the exhausted flame expired.

That was not all. Lívia's wisdom had foreseen the ordeals the marriage would have brought her. When all had calmed down in his heart, Félix naively confessed to himself that the breach in his love, as painful as it had been, was yet the most reasonable solution. The doctor's love experienced posthumous doubts. With the passing of years, the veracity of the letter that had prevented their marriage not only seemed possible to him, but even probable. One day Meneses told Félix he had ultimate proof that Luís Batista had written the letter. Not only did Félix refuse his testimony, he did not even ask what proof he had. He thought to himself that, even without Batista's vileness, the verisimilitude of fact could not be excluded, and that alone assured him of his rectitude.

The widow's solitary, austere existence did not quell Félix's suspicious spirit, although he believed in it at first. With time, though, he doubted she had simply taken refuge. He believed it was dissimulation.

With all of the means available to be fortunate, by society's standards, Félix is essentially unhappy. Nature placed him among the class of men who are pusillanimous and visionary, whom the poets describe as "losing the good for fear of seeking it." Not content with happiness surrounding him, he wants to obtain a different intimate, lasting, and consoling affection. He never will. Although resurrected for a few days, his heart has left any sense of trust and memory of illusion forgotten inside its grave.

[1] In Portuguese speaking societies, this use of *doctor* is a social, rather than linguistic quirk. The term *doctor* followed by the given name is a generic honorific, usually meaning the individual has attended university, but in some instances, is a mere show of respect. It so happens that Doctor Félix did attend medical school, but other males, who are not M.D.s, also receive this style.

[2] Laranjeiras is a neighborhood with lush vegetation in the southern part of the city of Rio de Janeiro. The Guanabara Palace, one time residence of Princess Isabel (1865–1889), as well as President Getúlio Vargas (1937–1945), is located there. In the mid to late nineteenth century, when the novel takes place, it was a wealthy neighborhood occupied by villas.

[3] The Shield of Achilles is from the epic poem *Iliad* (book 18, lines, 478-608), about the Trojan War, by the Greek poet Homer (late eighth-early seventh century BC). Achilles lends his shield to his friend Patroclus, who is killed in battle. Achilles then goes into battle with a new shield his mother has requested from the god Hephaestus. As described in the poem, the shield's elaborate decoration—a series of concentric circles depicting the earth, sky, sun, agriculture, livestock, dancing, and cities at war and at peace—has been interpreted as a microcosm of the existence of everyman. The shield is forged in bronze, tin, gold and silver. Machado de Assis's reference to "tin and gold" may be a metaphor for the strength and weakness inherent to mankind.

[4] Louis-Henri Murger (1822–1861) was a French novelist best known for *Scènes de la vie de bohème*, an inspiration for Puccini's opera, *La Bohème*.

[5] The form of address *colonel* may refer to a military title, but it was also used as a generic honorific, mainly for large landholders (many of

165

whom were officers in the National Guard, a militia that existed from 1831–1922).

[6] Tijuca, a district in the northern part of the city of Rio de Janeiro, is home to one of the largest urban forests in the world. In the mid-sixteenth century the Jesuits resided there, where they cultivated sugar. When they were expelled in the mid-eighteenth century, the elevated, relatively cooler lands were leased to wealthy families, who built villas. By the turn of the nineteenth century, several industries including textiles, hats, beer, tobacco, and canned goods were established in Tijuca, and many of the mansions were transformed into residences and hotels.

[7] In the original (1872), the noun *moleque* referred to an enslaved young man of African descent. Slavery was abolished in Brazil in 1888. Over time *moleque* has evolved to refer to any male child, often mischievous.

[8] Portuguese poet Francisco Sá de Miranda (1481–1558) initially wrote works traditional to the Portuguese language, such as cantigas and trovas. Later, influenced by his travels in Italy and Spain, he introduced Renaissance forms to Portugal, the sonnet and the eclogue. His well-known plays *Estrangeiros* (staged in 1528) and *Vilhalpandos* (1530/1531) were comedic satires, critical of contemporary society.

[9] *Dia da Gloria* is the celebration of the Roman Catholic belief in the assumption of the Virgin Mary, body and soul, into heaven. This holiday is celebrated, sometimes with a feast, on August 15th.

[10] Minas Gerais is a large, relatively wealthy inland state in the southeast of Brazil. As its name indicates—meaning *general mines*—it is mineral rich. Gold and diamonds were discovered in the late seventeenth and early eighteenth centuries. The wealth generated by mining led to a sophisticated production and appreciation of architecture, music, and literature. From 1822 until 1891, when it became a state, it was a province in the Brazilian Empire. Gold and diamonds have been replaced by mining in iron ore, manganese, several other minerals, and agriculture.

[11] The tilbury is named after the London coachmaker Gregor Tilbury. Made to carry only two people, it is a light, single horse drawn carriage with two large wheels.

[12] Rocio (now Praça Tiradentes) was a plaza in the city center where the Real Teatro de São João was inaugurated in 1813. In addition to its bustling nightlife, it was also the location for government edicts, and corporal punishment. In the early 1800's, when he was still Prince Regent, Dom João VI had relocated the pillory to Rocio.

[13] Rua do Ouvidor is one of the oldest streets in Rio de Janeiro, located in the center of the city. Although it had gone by various names, in 1780, during colonial times, its current name was adopted to honor the judicial representative, or ombudsman, *Ouvidor-Mor* Francisco Berquó da Silvera, one of three appointed assistants to the Governo Geral. *Ouvidor*, meaning *Auditor* in English, is a fitting name for a street known as the news and gossip center of the colony. By the late nineteenth century, it was bustling with shops, cafés, bookstores and other attractions for the city's intellectuals and elites.

[14] *The Dardanian Fugitive* is a reference to the mythological Trojan hero King Aeneas, leader of the Dardans, who escaped Troy when it was sacked by the Greeks. He fled to Rome and became the progenitor of the Romans. He appears in Homer's *Illiad* as well as in Virgil's *Aenead*.

[15] *Dona*, followed by a given name, is a respectful form of address for adult women, regardless of marital status.

[16] In eighteenth century Brazil, according to Canon Law, the minimum age to be married was 14 years for males, 12 year for females. With Decree no 181 January 24, 1890 (Marriage Law), after the Republic was established, the ages shifted to 16 years for males, 14 years for females.

[17] Luís Vaz de Camões (1524–1580) is considered the greatest poet of the Portuguese language. *The Lusiads* (1572) is an epic poem narrating the adventures of Golden Age Portuguese explorer Vasco da Gama's sea voyage to India. Leonardo, appearing in stanza 75, Canto IX when the sailors meet the Nymphs on paradisiacal Island of Love, is an oft disappointed flirtatious ladies' man who finds true love in that episode.

[18] Guanabara Bay (Baía de Guanabara) is the nineteen mile long, seventeen mile wide bay giving access to the port of Rio de Janeiro. Although having suffered severe environmental damage since it was first found by

Europeans in 1502, the large oceanic bay, with its over 130 islands, maintains much of its natural beauty. The cities of Niteroi and São Gonçalo are opposite to Rio de Janeiro, on the eastern shore.

[19] Botafogo is a beachside neighborhood located on a large circular inlet within Guanabara Bay. Although within the original municipal demarcation of 1565, it was only formally established as a district in 1590. With the arrival of the Portuguese royal family in 1808, like much of the city, Botafogo became increasingly urban. Mansions, home to minor nobles, British businessmen, and coffee barons were prevalent; the São João Batista cemetery was founded there in 1852, one of the first open to people from all social classes. Steamboat (1846) and trolley (1860) routes connecting the neighborhood to downtown Rio de Janeiro contributed to Botafogo's growth in population and social diversity.

[20] Kythera Island was the birthplace of Aphrodite, the goddess of love, according to the ancient Greek poet Hesiod, while Daniel Defoe's *Robinson Crusoe*'s eponymous castaway survived alone on his island.

[21] Previously, the host of the party is referred to as *colonel*; here, as *counselor*, indicating the character is a politician or diplomat.

[22] Catumbi, like Laranjeiras and Tijuca, is a neighborhood in Rio de Janeiro. It is located in the center of the city and is one of the oldest districts. At the time—in contrast to the twenty-first century—it was an elegant neighborhood, populated by the well-heeled.

[23] Like the previously mentioned male house servant, this female household servant (*mucama* in the original) is enslaved.

[24] The Carceler was an ornately decorated tea room and ice cream parlor located on Rua Direita, one of the original thoroughfares of Rio de Janeiro and, during the nineteenth century, among the most important. It was a very popular meeting place among those who could afford it.

[25] Rua do Lavradio is located in Lapa, a district in the center of Rio de Janeiro. Machado de Assis lived in Lapa for most of 1874. One of the oldest streets in the city, Rua do Lavradio is named for the 2nd Marquess of Lavradio (1727–1790; 11th Viceroy of Brazil, 1769–1779), who built

a mansion there, where he entertained lavishily. Through the mid nineteenth century, theaters, cafés, and restaurants occupied the street. By the
late nineteenth century, its heyday had come to an end.

[26] This household servant—again *mucama* in the original—would have
been a enslaved girl in charge of the child. In Brazil, as in the U.S., the
enslaved domestic girls who took care of their masters' offspring were
often no more than children themselves.

[27] Autograph books were a centuries old tradition, originally among stu-
dents who would sign each other's by way of holding on to friendships.
The custom came in and out of fashion in Europe and the Americas. By
the late nineteenth century, they were mainly used by girls and women
to gather signatures, messages, quotations and drawings from their family and friends. It is not clear where Lívia's came from, but since she had
lived for a time in Minas Gerais, she may have started her book upon
leaving Rio de Janeiro.

[28] This tongue-in-cheek comment is a reference to *Le Parnasse
Contemporain*, an anthology of poetry published in France (1866, 1869,
prior to the publication of *Ressurreição*, and again in 1876). Its contribu-
tors included Stéphane Mallarmé and Paul Verlaine. The title of the book
referred to Mount Parnassus, home of the muses of Greek mythology.
The Parnassian movement had followers in Brazil from the 1880s until
the arrival of the Modernist movement in 1922. It was influenced in
part by the philosopher Arthur Schopenhauer, whose ideas were also
important to Machado de Assis. Although Machado de Assis's novels are
innovative and unique, his poetry, of which he published four volumes,
Crisálidas (1864), *Falenas* (1870), *Americanas* (1875) and *Ocidentais*
(1880) was less so. Nonetheless, his poetry reveals extreme attention
to the brevity of form he perfected in his novels, especially *Memórias
Póstumas de Brás Cubas* (1881) and *Dom Casmurro* (1899).

[29] This is a reference to Aesop's fable, "The Frogs who Desired a King," in
which frogs, having no leader, called upon Zeus to provide one. Instead
of a king, Zeus threw down a log. The still unsatisfied frogs called upon
Zeus again, who sent either a water snake or heron (depending on the
version of the fable) that proceeded to eat them.

[30] In the original, the word for "estate" is *chácara*. This term was used for properties set in a large garden, often including a fruit grove. In nineteenth century Rio de Janeiro, like in other cities around the world, people owned homes with what we would now consider a great deal of land, a few acres. The word *chácara* is still used interchangeably to indicate a house, its outdoor space or both, but nowadays usually in reference to non-urban property of indeterminate size.

[31] Rio de Janeiro is still the Capital of the State of Rio de Janeiro, but the reference here is to Rio de Janeiro as the Capital of Brazil, which it was from the time of independence in 1822 until 1960 when, under President Kubitscheck, the Capital was transferred to Brasilia, the newly built Federal District in the center-western region of Brazil.

[32] This expression is an ironic reference to French poet François Villon's (c 1431–c 1463) ballad celebrating famous historical and mythological women, *Ballade des femmes du temps jadis* whose interrogative refrain, *Où sont les neiges d'antan* (*Where are the snows of yesteryear*, as translated by Dante Gabriel Rosetti, 1828–1882), has been borrowed in literature and music, including by Bertolt Brecht (1898–1956), Tennessee Williams (1911–1983), and Julian Fellowes (b 1949). Machado de Assis also used his version, *Onde estão elas, as flores de antanho* (*Where are they, the flowers of yesteryear*) in his later novel *Memórias Póstumas de Brás Cubas* (1881).

[33] This is an affectionate term in French, meaning *my pal*, a flip indication, socially inappropriate at the time, that Cecília and Félix had been intimate.

[34] Jacques Offenbach (1819-1880) was German born composer and cellist who settled in Paris after studying there at the conservatory of music. He was a talented musician and also prankster, known for his *opera buffa* compositions (comedic, at times risqué operettas). In addition to drawing from contemporary surroundings (*La vie Parisian* 1866), Offenbach used parody and satire to depict the court life of Napoleon III and to retell stories from Greek mythology.

[35] Carl Maria von Weber (1786–1826) was a German composer, pianist, guitarist, and conductor. He wrote operas in the German Romantic tradition, as well as Catholic religious music.

[36] The term *opera buffa* was first used to describe comedic Italian opera in the early 1700's whose themes were taken from daily life, as distinguishable from *opera seria* (serious opera). Prior to developing as its own genre, *opera buffa* were often short interludes in *opera seria*.

[37] Here again Luís Batista brings up a risqué, suggestive topic. Along with Eve, Bathsheba is the only other female whose nudity was traditionally acceptable in Christian art. According to the Hebrew Bible, Bathsheba, the wife of Uriah, was bathing when she was seen by King David from his rooftop. He became enamored and had her brought to him. She became pregnant and King David sent Uriah into battle, and he was killed. The death of King David and Bathsheba's first child, the result of the adulterous relationship, was considered God's punishment. Their son Solomon, however, eventually became king, making Bathsheba the Queen Mother.

[38] It is agreed among biblical historians that King David, of the united monarchies of Israel and Judah, existed around 1000 BCE. He is the very same David who fought Goliath. In some gospels he is described as a forebear of the Messiah.

[39] According to the gospels of Mark, Mathew, and Luke, Simon of Cyrene was ordered by Roman soldiers to help Jesus carry his cross to his crucifixion. He was a bystander who had traveled from Cyrene, in northern Africa (now Libya) to Jerusalem, probably for Passover. There is some debate over whether Simon may have already been sympathetic to Jesus at the time of the Crucifixion. Simon of Cyrene is a depicted in the fifth station of the cross.